WHISPERS OF LOVE IN SWEETWATER SPRINGS

JOSIE RIVIERA

This book is dedicated to all my wonderful readers who have supported me every inch of the way.
THANK YOU!

5 STAR READER REVIEWS

Review by N. Jean:
5.0 out of 5 stars
"Ms. Riviera's reputation for writing clean, wholesome romance stories continues with her new book. It is refreshing to know that you can pick up any of her books and feel confident that there will be no offensive scenes."

Amazon Review by M. Fouraker:
5.0 out of 5 stars
"Josie Riviera kicks off a new series with Whispers of Love in Sweetwater Springs. This is more than her usual sweet romance - she has sprinkled a bit of mystery into her story. Long-time readers who appreciate her clean romances can rest assured that this book still meets those standards. The addition of a romantic mystery sweetened the pot and kept me guessing at the solution up until the very end."

Review by M.Mier:
5.0 out of 5 stars
"I could not put this book down, really enjoyed it!!"

AUTHOR ENDORSEMENT

Whispers of Sweetwater Springs is a delightful trio of cozy mysteries set in the small town of Sweetwater Springs the author beautifully brings to life!

Whispers of Love features Bookstore owner Olivia who must find the truth behind a secret letter found between the pages of a book. Will she also rekindle a relationship with her childhood sweetheart?

In *Whispers of Maple Memories* Nora is compelled to investigate the secrets of a hidden map marked with an X, but will she also find love?

Whispers of Holiday Magic features bakery owner Emma who uncovers a mysterious photograph. In seeking the truth will Emma discover love?

New York Times Bestselling Author Laura Scott

ACKNOWLEDGMENTS

An appreciative thank you to my patient husband, Dave, and our three wonderful children.

CHAPTER 1

"*Y*ou've got to be kidding me! Only two boxes of books when I ordered three?" Olivia Harper's exasperated voice echoed through the cozy confines of *Harper's Haven*, the bookshop she'd inherited from her grandfather Elijah.

She hoisted the books inside and shook her head. "I guess I'll have to charm my customers with my dazzling personality instead of relying on the books."

With a grin and a sigh, she reached for her cell phone to rectify the mistake. Sunlight filtered through the lace curtains, casting a glow over the antique furniture and over-stuffed chairs. The scent of aged paper and rich mahogany embraced her like an old friend.

Blooming cherry blossom trees, with slender upright branches and rounded canopies, lined the street. When she finished her phone call, she opened the window to let in the floral-scented air.

As she gazed around her shop, a flicker of uncertainty passed through her.

Harper's Haven wasn't just a bookstore—it was her dream,

her legacy. She had poured her heart and soul into every detail, determined to carry on her grandfather's proud tradition. But lately, the weight of responsibility seemed more burdensome than ever.

With each passing year, the pressures of running the business grew more daunting.

She shrugged off her khaki-colored windbreaker, hung it on a hook by the door, and secured an apron over her clothes. Then she kneeled beside the book shipments and sliced through the packing tape.

She lifted out two hardbound editions of *Wuthering Heights*, their gold-leaf lettering glinting in the gauzy morning light.

The distinct tinkle of the shop bell was unmistakable, and she greeted the first customer of the day.

But no one responded.

"Hello?" she called out again. "Can I help you find anything?"

Only silence. Every aisle lay empty and still.

Okay, this was strange. She was certain she had heard the bell.

"Anyone here?" She repeated.

Nope. No reply. She must've been mistaken. She was obviously alone.

Corralling her unease into something more productive, she redirected her attention to her task. As she sliced through the packing tape on the next box, a flash of creamy parchment grabbed her attention. She crouched for a better look, clearing dust bunnies from the wooden floorboards. An envelope lay slightly hidden underneath the front door.

She yanked the envelope free. The texture was luxuriously thick, and clearly expensive stationery. No postage, no address … only a wax seal, keeping its contents mysteriously confined. The wax itself was an unusual shade of yellow, its sheen catching the morning light streaming through the windows.

There were no clues as to the sender, an intriguing omission.

Her fingertip dipped over fancy lettering.

The initials L.B.

Where had she seen that unique script before, with its elongated curves and artistic loops? It tugged at her memory but hovered slightly out of reach.

The letter was addressed to:

Ms. Lillian Beaumont

Sweetwater Springs

Whispers of Love

"Whispers of love?" she asked aloud. "What does it mean?"

The handwritten style was antiquated but graceful, with long, sweeping strokes. All perfectly precise except for the initial L, elongated by a slight wavering in an otherwise steady hand.

As Olivia flipped the envelope, a tiny drawing made her breath still. A single heart flanked Lillian's name, colored a vivid red.

Lillian Beaumont was a woman in her 70s. She had recently moved back to Sweetwater Springs, having been gone for decades. Elegant and from an esteemed family, she lived on her inherited estate at the edge of town.

Her silver hair was always perfectly styled. She favored classic pieces in luxurious fabrics—cashmere sweaters in soft pastels, pencil skirts, and her signature red lipstick. On occasion, she perused Olivia's bookshop and purchased armfuls of classic books.

Although, come to think of it, Olivia hadn't seen Lillian in several weeks.

She straightened.

In her peripheral vision, she caught a flicker of motion behind her—the swish of a coat, an odd shuffle of footsteps quickly fading.

Envelope still in hand, she wandered down the aisle.

"Hello? May I help you find anything?"

Again, nothing. The silence seemed to press in on her, heavy and unsettling.

She retreated and ran her fingertip over the wax seal, specks of it breaking off, then placed the envelope on the counter.

As she unloaded the remaining shipments, her thoughts drifted to the unexplained letter. Who was it from, and why deliver it in such a cryptic way? The hand-drawn heart suggested Lillian had a secret admirer.

The morning passed quickly with a steady stream of customers, while Olivia dusted off shelves, lit several scented candles, and cashed out book sales.

The sunny spring weather had apparently put everyone in high spirits and in a buying mood. She helped Mrs. Dalton select a few gardening books to start planning her summer vegetable garden. She also set aside a couple of new young adult fantasy novels for two teenage girls to pick up.

At noon, Emma Jacobsen, who owned *Blissful Bites*, the bakery next door, stopped by. As usual, she was dressed to the nines despite her flour-dusted apron. Emma often came to chat when business was slow. She was in her late twenties, with fair skin and glowing, rosy cheeks.

"I'm done for the day and headed home," Emma announced. Her blond hair fell to her shoulders in loose waves, impervious to frizz or the hairnet she often wore.

"You sold all of your baked goods already?" Olivia asked.

"Every single one, but I saved a chocolate donut for you." Emma handed Olivia a donut wrapped in wax paper.

"Thank you and enjoy the rest of your afternoon," Olivia smiled. "I don't close until six o'clock."

"But I start preparing fresh dough and baking before sunrise, so I work more hours than you."

"I don't know about that." Olivia gave Emma a mischievous jab and took a bite of her donut, thinking about the extra hours she spent on inventory management and curating book selections.

In her typical brazen fashion, Emma's gaze flew to the envelope on the counter. "What ... do we have here?" Her tone shifted to a higher pitch.

While Olivia recounted the story, an almost imperceptible shift appeared in her friend's appearance.

Emma grimaced and touched her neck. "Possibly it's one of Lillian's secret fans." She shifted from one foot to the other. "You always had a knack for solving puzzles when we were young. I'm sure you'll be able to figure it out."

"Lillian Beaumont hasn't dated in ages. Word is, she never married."

"It's never too late for love." Emma's shoulders hunched. "At least for you. Not for me."

"Don't say that."

"I'm still struggling to run the bakery after my mother's passing. That's enough excitement for me."

"You have the option to hire help to reduce your workload," Olivia replied.

"Like you? You've never done anything of the sort."

Olivia shrugged. "I'm fine."

"So am I, and I'll run the bakery alone. My mother and grandmother did, and I'm carrying on their legacy."

A legacy of overwork, Olivia thought, though she kept silent. Emma wouldn't trust her bakery to anyone else. Her grief over her mother's unexpected death had stopped her from moving forward with her life.

Olivia grabbed a bottle of water from behind the counter and drank several sips. "So, you and I are currently dateless."

"Seems that way."

In truth, Olivia longed for a partner, a man to share her passions and support her dreams. She yearned for the warmth of love and the comfort of a family. However, exactly like Emma, fear held her back. Fear of change, fear of letting someone in, fear of losing the one constant in her life —her cherished bookshop.

"Maybe a handsome, heroic guy will move into town for you," Emma said.

"He better move in soon." Olivia smiled. "Or at least before I hit the age of thirty."

"Hey, if it's not too late for Lillian, then it's definitely not too late for you." Emma tapped her fingers on the counter. Nevertheless, there was more to her words—something lurking just below the surface. "The letter writer might be someone closer than you think."

As they swapped speculations, Emma's attentiveness carried a deliberate edge as she adjusted her denim skirt and fidgeted with her hair.

Did she know something? Or was she merely playing along with the intrigue?

Though they contrasted in looks, with Emma's petite frame and blond locks differing from Olivia's willowy height and chestnut curls, their friendship had always worked. As different as sunrise and sunset, each woman admired talents in the other she herself did not possess, and, despite her odd behavior, Emma was a true and reliable friend.

With a quick goodbye, Emma headed back to her bakery to close for the day, with promises to sleuth out ideas about the letter writer.

Although the bookshop kept Olivia busy for the next hour, her thoughts took a detour. Underneath her cheerful demeanor, a deep longing for companionship and love had taken root. She wanted someone to share her experiences, her interests, and the quiet moments that made life worth living.

Work had become her sanctuary, a refuge where she had the opportunity to lose herself in stories, and vicariously experience the affection she craved. Yet, as fulfilling as her work was, it was unable to fill the void in her heart.

Love would require a leap of faith, a willingness to risk her carefully cultivated independence, and take a chance. The alternative—a life spent alone witnessing others discover their happily-ever-afters—seemed increasingly hollow.

Shaking off her melancholy thoughts, she resumed the task at hand. She couldn't help but wonder if the mysterious letter held a clue to Lillian's own journey with love. Perhaps, in unraveling the secrets of the past, Olivia might stumble upon the courage to open her heart to the possibilities of the future.

She looked forward to catching up with Lillian. The woman's wit and sophistication always brightened Olivia's day.

Should she notify her about the strange delivery?

Yes, of course. The letter was addressed to her, and the contents were none of Olivia's business. She should personally deliver the letter to Lillian.

Then again, maybe not. Olivia sought to respect the privacy of the letter's sender as well as that of the recipient. More importantly, directly approaching Lillian without understanding the context or the sender's intentions could be intrusive.

Olivia ran her fingers across the weighty parchment. The meticulously drawn heart suggested strong emotions.

When the time was right, she'd approach Lillian in a

thoughtful and considerate manner, planning the conversation to ensure a positive and supportive interaction.

She tucked the letter in her apron pocket for safekeeping and decided to observe Lillian closely at their next meeting before springing the letter on her. Perhaps there would be unspoken clues—a blush, a tearful glimmer in her eye—to expose whether joyous news or old heartaches might wait within the envelope. For now, the contents remained unknown.

The shop bell jangled, and the front door swung open.

Olivia looked up, a greeting frozen on her lips.

Her childhood friend stood in the doorway, his hazel eyes glinting beneath his artfully tousled dark hair.

She grabbed the counter to steady herself, hoping her knees wouldn't give out.

"Daniel Whitfield. Is it really you?" The question ran from her lips. Her pulse thumped in her ears, resembling an erratic drumbeat. She studied his handsome face, searching for traces of the boy she had once known.

Their gazes locked, and the seconds hung suspended. His athletic build and broad shoulders filled out a well-fitted leather jacket. His wavy hair framed a face that had grown more chiseled and defined since their teenage years.

He summoned images of long ago afternoons spent sharing books, floating into imaginary worlds, and eating chocolate-chip cookies. Her favorite, she'd declared. Especially if they had lots of chocolate chips.

"Loads," he always assured her when he handed her a store-bought cookie. His grin suggested that he might've sneaked in a few extra chips when she wasn't looking.

Daniel had been her best friend and appreciated her shy introspection.

He got her. He understood her.

They passed countless summer evenings chasing fireflies

and stargazing, dreaming about the lives they would someday lead.

When they grew into their teens, she developed an insatiable crush on him. She thought of him always and everywhere, even when they weren't together. She assumed he felt the same when they shared their first kiss.

But then he was gone, awarded a scholarship to a prestigious college in another state, aspiring to become a historian and preservationist specializing in museum studies.

"I'm planning to travel the world, Ollie," he told her. "But someday I'll be back."

And she was left in Sweetwater Springs. Alone. And he hadn't come back.

He promised to stay in touch, though he never had, save for a few postcards and hasty letters.

Seeing him in person after all these years, his unexpected appearance only amplified the warring emotions inside her.

His achievements in international projects that integrated history and preservation techniques had led to frequent media appearances. She'd seen his interviews on television and online.

"Hi," he said quietly. He stepped further into the shop, and anticipation fluttered in her chest. His presence filled the room, commanding, yet reassuring, like a warm cuddle on a chilly day. He came closer, his gaze never leaving hers. "You look great."

She fine-tuned the buttons on her cream blouse. She had paired the blouse with a floral skirt, accessorized by Grandma Rachel's pearl necklace. Classic clothing in the old Hollywood style suited her better than mass produced modern fashion. The styles had histories. Similar to her books.

Though today she didn't feel stylish. Today, she felt self-conscious.

Perhaps, if she was well-traveled.

But she wasn't, and he was.

"Thanks. You're not so bad yourself." She felt a blushing warmth travel up her cheeks, and she silently hoped that the sunlight through the window wouldn't betray her reaction to his closeness.

Sporting his signature crooked smile, he embraced her in a long, tender hug. His masculine scent mixed with leather and an intoxicating foreign spice—something new and spicy —and more evidence of the success she'd admired from afar.

She inhaled traces of the familiar, clean, and fresh, uniquely him. It brought back a flood of memories, of stolen kisses and whispered promises of a love that had never faded.

The strength of his arms offered security, a quiet acknowledgement of the years they'd spent apart. She pressed her face into his chest, unable to resist, and noticed his heart quickening ever so slightly.

"It's so good to see you, Ollie," he murmured in her ear, sending a tingle down her spine. "Real, real good." His hands rested on her shoulders, igniting memories of their long-held connection.

Ollie. The nickname was a nod to their shared history, an affectionate shorthand, like slipping into a well-worn pair of shoes. He hadn't forgotten.

She met his hazel eyes, reflecting intelligence, kindness, and longing. Tiny flecks of gold danced in their depths. And something more—a hidden gravity she couldn't fully decipher.

"You haven't called me Ollie since we were kids." She swept back a chestnut curl escaping from her updo, silently cursing her unruly hair for choosing this moment to stage a rebellion.

"Concrete proof it's been far too long." His eyes twinkled with mirth, though his voice was low and smooth. "I hope you haven't outgrown your affection for socks that don't match."

"Never," she replied.

Once upon a time, they confessed things to each other. He once had a dream of being able to fly, so real that he'd been disappointed when he woke up and realized it wasn't true. She always wore mismatched socks for good luck, and it had become a personal superstition.

Today she wore one red and one blue sock. Some superstitions died hard.

Affection enveloped her from head to toe as she soaked in his good-looking features. His face carried a touch of rugged individuality, and his jawline was peppered with a dark stubble that lent him an air of casual sophistication. The radiance of his smile had the power to brighten even the darkest corners of her heart.

Time had certainly changed everything. In the past, he was her confidante.

But now. Now things were different—even more intimate.

"I've returned to settle down in this town permanently." He lifted her chin. "Are you pleased?"

She studied his face, searching for the boy she had once known. She took in the man he had become, a heady mix of awareness and novelty that left her both exhilarated and unbalanced. "If your words hold true, then undoubtedly."

"They are true." The curve of his lips radiated genuine understanding. "Think you can catch up on things around Sweetwater Springs?" He gestured toward the door. "Possibly over lunch?"

"I already ate a chocolate donut."

"A donut isn't lunch."

"For me, it is, though I might be able to clear my schedule for an old friend on a different day."

"I plan to be more than an old friend." As he scanned a shelf of historical fiction, his hand covered hers, where it rested on the polished oak surface of the counter. "Remember when we said we'd marry each other if we weren't able to find anyone better?"

"We used to joke about it. So, you didn't hit the jackpot?"

"Nope. You?"

"Nope." Her stomach fluttered, and she quickly changed the subject as she gazed across her shop—anywhere but at him. Every corner held a piece of her heart, from the eclectic array of books to the elegant retro seating.

"What brings you here today?" she asked.

"You."

"Me? I'm hardly a jackpot." She laughed, a bit too loudly. "You moved back to Sweetwater Springs several weeks ago."

"Ah, you've been checking up on me?"

"No."

Well, yes. In this modest town of ten thousand, news waltzed faster than the eye could blink.

"I was busy buying a house on Windsor Boulevard," he said. "An old Victorian."

"Ooh. Quite a posh street." Her comment carried a hint of good-humored recognition, a nod to the world they had once dreamed about.

Daniel chuckled. "Windsor Boulevard seemed fitting. A bit different from the old neighborhood."

Olivia detected a blend of ambition and desire in his words.

"You did it," she said. Despite his humble upbringing, he'd continually expressed a wish to reside on a more affluent street.

"Right." He shifted. "Like I mentioned, I came here to see

you. Plus, I met with the historical society about an upcoming exhibition, and it's only a half block away."

"Don't put yourself out."

He grinned. His hand still covered hers. His other hand reached for a leather-bound book on a shelf near the counter. "Hey, your shop is incredible—a reading corner and a brass chandelier. You've upgraded since your grandfather owned it."

Her shop wasn't solely a bookstore; it was a charming haven, nestled in the heart of Sweetwater Springs. Whenever she stepped inside, she marveled at how it always felt like coming home.

Visions of couples browsing the shelves for romantic reads, snuggled in the leather armchairs by the fireplace, brought a smile to her face. The antique volumes, with their tales of adventure, mystery, and timeless love, never failed to cast their spell over everyone who loved to read.

"Thanks. A lot can happen in ten years." Olivia drew back her hand. "You're welcome to look around. I have a fiction section and a shelf full of thriller novels."

She gestured to a reading nook nestled between two towering bookcases and studied his profile when he turned. Sunlight from the front window glinted off his dark, tousled hair, the color of espresso. His eyes glittered with an inquisitive spark, which she recalled from their childhood adventures scouring the countryside for magical creatures drawn from fairy tales. Whether in Sweetwater Springs or abroad, his lively imagination had led him to pursue a career safeguarding the rich history and architecture of the past.

After he slid a worn Agatha Christie book onto a shelf, he turned fully toward her, his desire softening his gaze.

Her breath snagged as his fingers swept away a stray wisp of hair that had fallen across her cheek. That rebellious hair again.

His fleeting touch had sparks leaping over her skin. She looked down, suddenly fascinated by the intricate pattern of the hardwood floor.

"I'm glad we finally have a chance to catch up, Ollie."

"Me, too." She missed him. His return was like a sucker punch to the gut, so unexpected yet so wonderful, and there was no hope for it.

"Do you remember the last time we saw each other?" he asked. "That summer evening by the lake, before I left for college?"

"How could I forget? We made a multitude of plans, dreamed endless dreams."

"I'm sorry it took me so long to return."

When she didn't respond, he stepped back and flipped through the pages of a well-known bestseller. "Remember when we used to go on treasure hunts?"

"Of course." She gave a slight dip of her head. "Or our hush-hush codes and messages?"

"Mirror writing. And our underground scripts and cipher pies."

"Definitely the best," she agreed.

"Are you keeping any secrets these days, Ollie?"

"Like what?"

"Any guy I should be aware of?" He pointedly stared at her left hand.

She was ringless.

"None. Though actually …" Olivia debated whether to involve him in her discovery of the puzzling letter. His passion for discovering concealed artifacts might be beneficial.

She retrieved the envelope and recounted the peculiar delivery.

"Whispers of Love? It sounds like the title of a romantic poem. And the heart drawing. Perhaps the sender had a special connection to Lillian." Daniel examined the letter, noting the expensive stationery and calligraphy spelling of Lillian Beaumont's name. "I remember her well. She once caught us trying to sneak a peek at her famous rose garden. I worried that she'd never stop scolding us."

"We were quite the mischievous duo, weren't we? I'm surprised that she didn't ban us from her property forever."

"Have you spoken to her about the letter?"

"Not yet. I wanted to observe her first in case the contents were sensitive."

"I'd be happy to partner on your little investigation if you'll have me. For old time's sake?" His eyes held an adventurous sparkle that Olivia well remembered.

"I'd love that." She swallowed the lump in her throat for all the years that had gone by without him, then tucked the letter back in her apron pocket.

Some things never changed. Their enduring bond of friendship and comradery transcended time. They weren't only discussing solving a mystery, they were rediscovering their love of a shared undertaking.

As he turned to leave, promising to be in touch, the bell jingled, its ring unusually sharp and insistent.

They traded a startled look.

He yanked the door open, surveying the cobblestone sidewalk as Olivia joined him.

The town's postcard-perfect street stretched before them. Locally owned businesses were painted in earthy tones, complementing the natural beauty of the surroundings. Potted plants sat outside in vivid purple and pink colors, a stark contrast against the subdued architecture. Spring had arrived in the Pacific Northwest, awakening the scenic mountain community from its winter slumber.

This was her favorite season, when the promise of fresh beginnings wrapped her world in an optimistic glow.

A beam of sun struggled to pierce impenetrable clouds. Yet the street seemed frozen in a silent scene, as if the entire town had taken a collective pause. The only sounds were the occasional creak of a road sign or the hum of a far-off car engine.

Olivia twisted one of the pearls on her necklace, the smoothness comforting to the touch. "Where is everyone?" she whispered.

"At lunch?" Daniel half-joked, although his lips tightened. "Your shop bell rang, right?"

"I heard it as loudly as you did." Goosebumps prickled her skin despite the snug temperature of the bookshop. First the unexplained letter, now phantom bell ringers? This day was getting odder by the minute.

After his departure a few minutes later, Olivia busied herself tending to afternoon customers while mulling over potential clues. Every so often, her thoughts strayed to Daniel. His passion for discovering the buried stories of people, sometimes in precarious situations, mirrored her own love of books and mysteries.

She inhaled. The comforting mustiness of well-loved novels, the faint trace of vanilla-scented candles flickering on antique tables, added to the light floral fragrance of cherry blossoms drifting in through the open window. The scent always reminded her of almonds or marzipans.

Hours later, before she closed for the day, a final tinkling bell roused her as Mr. Theodore Weatherly ambled through the doorway. A distinguished face in Sweetwater Springs, Theodore had never married, vehemently asserting he preferred to live alone. He was a kindly retired poet, and well-known for his calm, observant nature, and talent for heartrending verses.

"Good evening, Olivia." Theodore's clear blue eyes creased behind his trademark round spectacles.

"I'm about ready to close," she reminded him, as she did every night around the same time.

"I know. I'm taking a stroll to catch the last rays and mingle with the night shadows. A little tango with the sunset and a potential chat with the neighborhood cats. Gotta keep these old bones in check." He chortled. "What are you up to?"

Olivia smiled at his characteristic whimsy; a fox-trot of words frequently accompanied his escapades.

With his shock of white hair, and an endless collection of colorful bow ties, he had a habit of strolling slowly while nodding approval of his surroundings, as if the town were his personal art gallery and he were the sole critic.

"Oh, I'm not up to much, Theodore." Olivia felt for Lillian's letter in her apron pocket. "Merely some intriguing mysteries to unfold."

Theodore swallowed hard, then waved a hand airily. "Ah yes, life does delight in its little enigmas." He trailed off, his eyes unfocusing as if lost in inflated memories.

"How well do you know Lillian Beaumont?" she blurted.

"Ah … beautiful, delightful Lillian." A tender smile graced his lips. "I used to know her well before she moved away."

"She moved back."

"I heard." He nodded, and she detected a quiver in his voice.

She wondered, not for the first time, what forgotten stories from past decades revolved around his discerning mind. He didn't inquire about her intriguing mystery, and she didn't expand on it. Apparently, he wasn't interested.

After a short interval, his smile returned.

"Alright, good night." Theodore turned on his heel. "I'm gonna check on my daughter's bakery next door."

Although not his biological daughter, Emma had become Theodore's daughter in spirit, his only family over the years. On many occasions, they spent holidays together.

Olivia wished the scenario would eventually change for Emma, wished she would be able to heal from her mother's passing. It didn't mean Emma should exclude Theodore from her life. It simply meant that she needed a healthy relationship with a man she could love.

"Emma closed her bakery after lunch," Olivia replied.

"I'll catch her tomorrow, then." Theodore drifted out the door, humming a romantic melody.

I Love You More Today Than Yesterday.

Sonny & Cher? Spiral Staircase? Olivia recognized the song immediately.

Bemused, she watched him go.

Theodore couldn't have a connection to the letter, could he?

Dismissing the possibility, Olivia retrieved the envelope. She examined the handwriting once more, searching for any trace to jog her memory.

Nope. Not a thing.

For the next ten minutes, she shelved the last few books, reluctant for the inviting refuge of her bookstore to go dim and silent.

The shop bell rang again, louder than usual, a sudden disruption rippling through the bookshop.

"Hello?" She tried to listen for more. Sounds. Footsteps. Anything. "Theodore? Sorry, but remember, I'm about to close?"

No one stood in the doorway.

The fine hairs on her arms lifted, as if invaded by tiny pushpins. The tidy space looked undisturbed; the books were organized on their appropriate shelves. However, she couldn't escape the uncanny sensation of invisible eyes watching her every move.

Flickering candlelight cast dancing phantoms along the

aging floorboards. She stepped over and blew out the candles.

Hastily, she gathered her belongings, removed her apron, and slid on her jacket. Each step resonated with the tick-tock of an old clock on the wall, its rhythm adding an ominous undertone to the otherwise peaceful environment.

As she walked outside to activate the security alarm and lock the front door, the letter crinkled softly in her pocket. Streetlamps fought a losing battle against the dense fog draping the town, the feeble glow barely making a dent.

An abrupt clatter of metal cans caused her to spin around. A figure limped out of the alley by the historical society building. As they straightened, she noticed the figure wore a black fedora.

The streetlight caught the wink of what appeared to be cigarette smoke.

Was it possible? Theodore? He was the last person she had seen.

As the figure limped out of sight, she tried to shake off her absurd suspicion. Theodore didn't limp. Theodore didn't smoke. Besides, why would the friendly poet be sneaking outside the historical society at this hour?

Then again, he did have a habit of evening wandering.

His connection to the letter was likely nothing. And yet, she wrestled with the idea that he knew more than he let on by his airy dismissal and unconcern.

As the other businesses dimmed their lights, the blossom-scented air took on an enigmatic quality, as if it cradled concealed secrets.

A gusty breeze tousled the awning of Emma's bakery. The chill seeped through Olivia's thin jacket as she headed to her apartment on Mistwood Lane.

Uneasy, she quickened her pace, resisting the urge to turn around.

She focused on the majestic outlines of snow-capped mountains in the distance, providing a stunning backdrop. This serene little town was a beautiful setting to call home.

Yet, a shiver traced a delicate path down her spine, refusing to be dismantled.

She scolded herself, banishing the urge to cower.

This was a perfect town.

Perhaps too perfect.

CHAPTER 2

*A*s the sun rose the following morning, Olivia prepared to enjoy her much-anticipated day off from the bustling world of her bookshop.

She slipped into a forest green wool coat, layering it over a cream-colored, cable-knit sweater and dark jeans, to shield against the Pacific Northwest chill. The contemporary casual atmosphere of her church allowed for a more relaxed dress code, and her choice of footwear was a pair of durable ankle boots. Around her neck, she wore a string of her grandmother Rachel's pearls, and tied her chestnut hair into a loose ponytail.

After attending a late morning service, she stepped outside.

The breeze was tinged with the distinct aroma of pine and the distant murmur of a stream.

Because the historical society building was closed on Sunday, Olivia stopped at the Sweetwater Springs library, housed in a grand brick building uptown. She intended to research and hopefully identify the writer of Lillian's letter. The society had a limited area to store documents since they had a smaller facility. The library offered additional space, including the attic.

Nora Winters, the town librarian, greeted Olivia and escorted her past the lofty shelves. The atmosphere held the well-known scent of used books, and the low hum of fluorescent bulbs provided a steady backdrop to the hushed tones of the library patrons.

"Are you here to join my book club?" Nora asked. "We have a new historical fiction novel set in World War II."

"Next month, I promise," Olivia replied. "April is a busy month for me."

Nora, a born and raised resident of Sweetwater Springs, was passionate about preserving the town's history, evident in the way she meticulously organized its collection. Her doe-like brown eyes conveyed both shyness and kindness. With her sandy-blond hair slicked back into a bun, she was the epitome of a bookish introvert. Although behind her introverted demeanor lay a wealth of knowledge and a deep love for literature.

As Olivia described her discovery of Lillian's letter, Nora's gaze expanded. A gleam of curiosity, perhaps? Or recognition?

It had only been one day since the letter had arrived, but Olivia suspected everyone.

"What a romantic notion, an anonymous admirer!" A rosy blush seeped up Nora's freckled cheeks. She adjusted her horn-rimmed eyeglasses and held the envelope up to the light. "I wonder who might've written such a letter?"

The million-dollar question. Too bad Olivia didn't have the million-dollar answer.

When Olivia asked for directions to the attic, Nora fiddled with the silver brooch pinned to her cardigan sweater, then wiped her hands along her knee-length tweed skirt.

"I shouldn't," Nora said. "The library's regulations bar public access."

"I won't be long. You've known me your whole life."

Nora glared at Olivia for a fleeting moment, as if she were battling an internal dilemma. However, Olivia decided she must've imagined it because, a moment later, Nora smiled.

As Olivia ascended the attic steps, dust particles floated in faded sunbeams. The musty air held confidences, like time traveling to the past.

When they reached the top of the stairs, Nora deposited the metal ring graced with a book-shaped fob into Olivia's palm.

Olivia studied the librarian's face. Behind the genial smile and bookish facade, Nora seemed filled with nervous energy, like a sentry guarding long-kept confidences. Her smile, which she still wore, didn't reach her eyes, and her gaze kept flickering to the staircase.

Olivia wondered if Nora knew the true significance of the letter and its ambiguous sender.

No, it wasn't likely. How could she?

However, there were hidden complexities beneath Nora's composed exterior. Perhaps her passion for archiving the town's history was tied to a personal connection from her own past. Perhaps a lost love? One never knew the stories etched in people's hearts.

Or she was simply worried about breaking the library's rules, costing Nora her job.

Olivia made a mental note to buy Nora a gift to show her gratitude for not following protocol. Beneath a guarded shell, Nora was a true kindred spirit who cared deeply for the townspeople, past and present.

The attic air was tinged with staleness, and the corners

were covered in cobwebs. Olivia shrugged off her coat, draped it on a table, and flicked on the lights.

She positioned a chair beside an aged trunk, rummaging beyond an ancient typewriter, inkwell, and quills to peek further inside. She discovered a well-preserved diary, whispers of a bygone era, and extracted it with care. The cover was made of cracked leather, its once vibrant hue faded to a mellow sepia tone.

The edges were delicately gilded and implied importance, as if the words held a value beyond everyday musings.

A small, ornate lock dangled from the side, and a tiny key, rusted but functional, lay beside it. The presence of a lock suggested the diary safeguarded confidences meant only for the eyes of its author.

The faint swish of yellowed pages filled the silent attic space as Olivia opened the diary. The pages overflowed with entries, the cursive handwriting revealing the author's intimate contemplations. Ink stains marked hurried inspiration or emotional outpouring, blots when the diarist may have paused to reflect on her thoughts.

Tucked between the pages were delicate, pressed flowers, their vibrant colors subdued by time. Each was a bird-like remembrance preserved between the lines of the author's narrative.

As Olivia reviewed the entries, a love story unfolded. The diarist was a woman from a prominent family, though her identity remained a mystery. Did she ever imagine that her private thoughts would be discovered in this public place?

The woman disclosed her romance with furtive notes and rendezvouses with an elusive man. Could this man hold the key to identifying Lillian's hidden devotee? Was the diarist related to Lillian herself?

However, there was no mention of Lillian's name.

Driven by interest, Olivia dove deeper into the historical

records and the town's founding families. She learned about how World War II had impacted the town—residents leaving for military service or industries connected to the war, causing shifts in the local economy. As the Pacific Northwest was known for its timber industry, logging activities boomed during wartime construction.

Then came the transition to peacetime economies in the 1950s, bringing home veterans adjusting to life after years of war.

How did all these pieces fit together? And how did any of this relate to Lillian?

Olivia searched for connections between past and present residents, tales of romance, heartbreak, and well-guarded revelations.

Though filled with intimate details, never once did the writer mention her own name. Instead, she referred to herself as "the diarist," keeping her identity unknown.

Olivia recognized her familiarity with the events described in the diary. There'd been a milestone celebration, and the opening of her grandfather's bookshop all those years ago.

Harper's Haven.

The diarist had met a handsome young man there and spent hours with him beneath the willow tree by the creek, the same spot where Olivia had shared special moments with Daniel.

As she continued to read, unease settled in her stomach. The entries alluded to a forbidden love, an affair that might have had significant repercussions for both the diarist and her mysterious paramour.

A sharp knock at the attic door startled Olivia. She jumped, the diary slipping from her hands and falling to the floor with a soft thud.

"Olivia?" Nora's voice called out from the other side of

the door. "I'm sorry, but I just received word that the library's board of directors is on their way for an impromptu visit. I'm afraid I'll have to ask you to leave for a few minutes."

Olivia's heart sank. Reluctantly, she gathered her belongings and made her way to the door.

As she stepped out of the attic, Nora's expression was apologetic but firm. "I can't risk the board finding out about this."

Olivia nodded, understanding Nora's position. However, as she descended the stairs, a troublesome consideration took hold. Why had the board chosen this particular moment to visit, especially on a Sunday? And why did Nora seem so nervous about their presence?

As Olivia reached the main floor of the library, she waited to see if she could catch a glimpse of the directors. Maybe their visit might provide insight into Lillian's letter and the diary.

Olivia wandered over to a shelf, browsing the titles while keeping a look out at the library's entrance.

After about fifteen minutes, the doors opened, and a group of five well-dressed individuals strode in. Three men and two women, all appearing to be in their late 50s or early 60s, carried an air of authority as they made their way toward the circulation desk.

Olivia recognized a few of the faces from town events and social gatherings. The tallest man, with salt-and-pepper hair and a neatly trimmed beard, was Dr. Elias Blackwell, a renowned surgeon who had recently retired. The woman to his right, wearing a tailored navy suit, was Linda Montgomery, a successful real estate developer.

As the board members engaged in a hushed conversation with Nora, Olivia strained to catch any snippets of their discussion. But their voices were too low, and the distance between them was too great.

Growing restless, Olivia took a closer look at the newspaper archives, hoping to find any articles that might mention Lillian or the mysterious diarist. She sifted through the pages, scanning the headlines for any relevant information.

A short article near the back of a decades-old edition snagged her attention.

'Local Businessman Donates Funds for New Library Wing,' the headline read.

She recognized the name of the donor:

Theodore Weatherly.

The article went on to praise his generosity and his dedication to the town's cultural heritage. But what struck Olivia was a brief mention of his close friendship with the Beaumont family, particularly Lillian's father, Arthur Beaumont.

She leaned back in her chair, her mind whirling with this new piece of information. She assumed he was Theodore's grandfather, judging from the date of the article.

A few minutes passed, and Nora signaled that it was all clear for Olivia to return to the attic.

Upon entering, she pulled up a chair. By the window, she carried on with her reading.

Many parts of the diary reflected events still occurring in Sweetwater Springs. The upcoming spring festival, held on the last Sunday of April, was an annual tradition, and a highlight on the town's yearly calendar. Potluck suppers in the community center were a monthly occasion, and residents brought their favorite homemade dishes.

Wasn't there a famous saying? The more things changed, the more they stubbornly clung to familiarity.

As she turned to the diary's last page, Olivia caught a phrase written in elegant cursive: *Whispers of Love.*

Whispers of Love.

A sharp inhale escaped her.

The words were written in a fine script, as if each letter had been chosen to convey a hidden sentiment. Recognition dawned as those three words jumped off the page, triggering an unspoken revelation.

This diary must belong to Lillian Beaumont. And whoever sent the letter knew those same three words meant something to her.

In the 1950s, societal expectations and class norms cited pressure on someone like Lillian, who came from a wealthy and influential family. These expectations included maintaining economic standing and marrying into a family of equal or higher status. Economic disparities between classes made it difficult for couples to express their feelings openly.

Was love a word that no one said out loud?

As Olivia dug deeper, her reflections glided to Daniel and the unexpected turn their lives had taken since his return to Sweetwater Springs. Having him in her life again, working alongside her to unravel the mystery of Lillian's letter, felt both thrilling and terrifying.

Once again, her old feelings of affection stirred. The memories of their shared childhood adventures, their love of literature, and the unspoken connection that had invariably drawn them together, were always there.

However, as adults, the stakes felt higher.

What would it mean for their relationship if they succeeded in solving the mystery? Would it bring them closer, or reveal truths that changed everything?

The secrets they uncovered might have far-reaching consequences, not only for Lillian, but for themselves as well. The past had a way of shaping the present, and their own story might become entangled with the lives of those who had come before them.

As she traced her fingers over the delicate pages of the diary, Olivia made a silent promise to herself. No matter what challenges lay ahead, or the truths they uncovered, she would face them head-on. And she hoped that Daniel would be by her side every step of the way.

She drew the attic curtains aside. The street below was lined with colorful houses and old-fashioned lamp posts. She spotted Daniel exiting *Pages and Aromas*, the café close by. He wore a charcoal-gray button-down shirt beneath an olive-green utility jacket and dark jeans.

Knowing him, he probably had attended an early church service, then volunteered at the local food bank, as he often did as a teen.

She lifted a creaking window and called out to him.

The inviting scent of oven-fresh croissants wafted upward from the café, a hint of coffee and cinnamon. The babble of pedestrians drifted in, intermingling with the strumming of a ukulele.

Delilah Fitzwater. Who else would play the ukulele on a Sunday afternoon in the middle of town?

With her vibrant personality and zest for life, Delilah was the town's eccentric local matchmaker. Ironically, she had never married. Today, she wore her typical attire—a riot of colors, featuring a purple feathered boa.

Daniel looked up at Olivia and grinned.

"How's the music?" she teased.

He gestured toward Delilah. "No one's better."

Delilah eyed them both, then began playing *Dream a Little Dream of Me*.

Olivia smiled and waved to Daniel. "Come join me!"

"I'll be right up." He crossed the street and approached the library.

If there was someone capable of unraveling this multi-layered mystery spanning generations, it was her longtime friend.

Well, no. He was more. Much more. But friend would do

for now.

CHAPTER 3

*D*aniel greeted Nora at the library check-out counter, then pointed to the stairs with a hasty explanation. As he stood on the threshold, he took a moment to catch his breath before joining Olivia by the window.

Sparse sunlight trickled in, painting fleeting patterns on the walls that exposed the hidden contours of books and collectibles.

"What's got you supercharged, Ollie?" His resonant voice broke the stillness.

She stood. "Lots of things."

"Like what?" His gaze settled on hers. She was a figure etched in memory. Her dark eyes, deep and expressive, met his. A willowy grace defined her silhouette, and chestnut strands of hair framed her face. Her features, delicate yet strong, radiated an understated, captivating allure.

"Like this." She handed him a diary, pointing to the last page where the words, *Whispers of Love* were written. "This is Lillian Beaumont's diary."

He perused the pages as if handling an ancient artifact. "Are you certain?"

"One hundred percent. And you won't believe this." She wrested an envelope from her purse and held it up. "Remember the letter?"

"Of course."

"Someone wrote those same three words here, and they addressed the letter to Lillian. *Whispers of Love*. There must be a connection."

His eyebrows scrunched together. He studied the sophisticated script and faded ink. "Lillian Beaumont," he mused aloud. "Her family was one of the most influential in Sweetwater Springs during the time she wrote in the diary, and her name still carries weight. What's the significance of those words?"

"Exactly what I'm asking."

"Is it a secret code? And why deliver the envelope to your bookstore, and not to Lillian herself?" He leaned closer to the window; lost in the vast expanse of the town below. Sweetwater Springs, with its delightful houses and winding streets, commanded untold stories that reverberated across decades.

The diarist's writings portrayed a clear depiction of a young woman torn between loyalty to her family and the yearning of her heart. Her words captured moments of sneak peeks and hidden meetings in undetected corners.

"Wow." Daniel fingered the leather cover. "She wasn't afraid to go against society's expectations for love."

"She kept everything under wraps." Olivia drew a breath. "We're entering a forbidden world."

"Her penmanship is lovely."

"And her words," Olivia added. "I can imagine her heart racing. The thrill of it all—it must've been an exciting time for her."

The diary spanned a six-month interval and alluded to furtive dates under the cover of moonlit nights. Lillian described the excitement she felt whenever she caught sight of the dynamic young man.

Daniel smiled. "The adult Lillian is so sophisticated."

"Imagine her seeing a guy without her mother's permission. I wonder if that's why she left ?" Olivia gave the diary a long, significant look. "For the life of me, I can't visualize Ms. Lillian doing anything that might raise an eyebrow. She is always so proper whenever I see her in the bookshop. She styles her silver hair perfectly, and she often dresses in an impeccably tailored suit."

"Ah, but keep in mind, beneath calm surfaces lie profound depths, Ollie. Maybe there's a wild side to the young Lillian the town never knew about."

Their retreat by the window caught the sunlight, creating a show of silhouettes across the forgotten treasures of the attic—rolled up maps tied with frayed ribbons, ancient ornate furniture covered by dusty sheets, and vintage photographs.

"It's easy for you to speculate, being that you're an experienced adventurer." Ollie outlined her chair's arm and didn't meet his eyes. "Some of us have always been predictable homebodies without a wild bone in their bodies."

"What's wrong with being a homebody?"

"Nothing, if you like ordinary."

"You're not ordinary, Ollie. And believe me, you're not predictable."

She offered a brisk smile. "I've been teased about my decision many times by my friends, but I still prefer to live in a small town."

"What did they say?"

"I should see the world and travel."

"You never left Sweetwater Springs?"

She shrugged. "Where would I go? I attended the community college here and earned a degree in business with a focus on entrepreneurship and management."

"Congratulations. Excellent choice."

"The degree served me well, with taking over the bookshop and all."

He appreciated the straightforwardness and authenticity in her statement.

"You also implemented outreach programs to promote a love for reading in underprivileged areas for elementary school-aged children," he said.

"Checking up on me?" She echoed his teasing words from the previous day.

He grinned. "Absolutely."

"In any case, I'm happiest as an armchair traveler." Her statement revealed a simplicity that Daniel found utterly endearing.

Despite her offhand response, he could've happily strangled every one of her so-called friends who had ever teased her.

Stopping an inch from her, he smoothed the grin from his face. "Predictable, huh? My dear homebody, you can find unpredictability in everyday encounters and jet-setting adventures."

"You went one way, and I went another. I only mentioned this because you and I were best buddies when we were young."

"We still are, I hope."

"Is that a question or a statement?"

He brushed his knuckles along her cheek. "A statement."

"We had big dreams, and you accomplished yours." Her voice was quiet.

"Never change, Ollie, and whatever you do, never sell yourself short. Everyone has different priorities and gifts. It's what makes this world unique." He drew her into his arms, grateful she didn't resist, that her body didn't tense. "I, for the record, have always had a thing for predictable homebodies."

"What kind of thing?"

He planted a loving kiss on her forehead. "This kind."

"The predictable kind?'

"Exactly." Daniel felt an intimate pull he couldn't ignore. He leaned in closer, his kiss conveying volumes of unspoken emotions.

The moment passed as she withdrew, and his thoughts scattered.

Olivia sat back in the chair she'd occupied earlier, picked up Lillian's diary, and began reading again. The worn leather creaked as she skimmed through the pages.

"Do you ever reflect on what might have been?" Her voice rose on the last three words. "If you had stayed in Sweetwater Springs, if we had …"

He took her hand, his fingers intertwining with hers.

"I think about it all the time," he admitted, his voice rough with emotion. "Leaving you was the hardest thing I've ever done. You had your own dreams, your own path to follow, and I had mine."

Tears formed at the corners of her eyes. "I never wanted you to leave," she whispered. "But I didn't know how to ask you to stay."

"I know." It was all he could say.

They went back to reading the diary.

Lillian's words painted a clear image of the sweetheart tree ceremony, a romantic event she yearned to share with her "special guy." The inked pages carried the burden of her forbidden wishes, desires, twirling on the edges of societal expectations.

Lillian's penned hopes collided with the harsh reality of familial expectations. She detailed the parental disapproval and ensuing tussles. Her parents, architects of her predetermined future, held a blueprint conspicuously excluding this "guy" in her life. The diary unfolded a narrative of love longing for expression, but tethered by the chains of cultural norms, leaving Lillian at the crossroads of heart and duty.

Daniel stood beside Olivia as she read.

"Listen to this passage." Olivia turned to a page toward the end of the diary. "'Tonight, I shall steal away to our gazebo in the woods, a hidden refuge where we first bared our hearts. To sit beside my beloved beneath the stars and moonlight is worth any risk.'" She looked up at Daniel. "Isn't that romantic?"

He let out an appreciative whistle. "The gazebo must've been quite special. I wonder if it's still there."

"I think I know where it is!" Olivia closed the window, then snatched the diary and her coat. "My friend and I saw an old gazebo years ago. It's close to one of the hiking trails in the woods. I'll bet it's Lillian's gazebo."

"What are we waiting for?" He gripped her hand and flicked off the lights. "Let's go."

A soft rustling sound caused him to glance down as a small slip of paper fell from the diary's pages. He bent to retrieve it and unfolded the note.

A single line appeared in faded, neat handwriting across the page:

"Meet me at the place where the willow weeps."

Olivia stared at him.

"Was the gazebo near a willow tree?" he asked.

She tucked the slip of paper and the diary in her tote bag. "I believe so."

The attic's ancient floorboards groaned in protest beneath their weight as they descended the staircase and offered a quick nod and thank you to Nora.

Daniel chose not to disclose to Nora the intention to

"borrow" the diary for a few days. He reasoned that since it appeared untouched for years, it wouldn't be missed.

Outside, a waft of wind coaxed a few blossoms to sway on budding branches. The sun hinted that spring was settling in for the long haul, and the fresh air filled Daniel's lungs, rich with potential.

Olivia took the lead, guiding him forward.

They started down a street that brought them to the edge of a forest. The faint song of birds and the occasional swish of unidentified creatures accompanied the crunching of leaves and twigs. Closer to the gazebo, a stream gurgled.

Dappled sunlight spilled through the dense canopy of ancient boughs. The air grew sweet with honeysuckle, melding with the earthy scent of moss and wildflowers.

"A few steps beyond this ridge!" Olivia exclaimed, a brisk lightness in her step.

Daniel glimpsed the battered stones and wood through a break in the trees, and a hitch in his breath caused him to hesitate. The tiny gazebo resembled a relic from a hidden garden, parts of it rusted, otherwise untouched by passing years. His fingers trailed over carvings of leaves and vines above the arched entrance. A weather-beaten wooden bench sat inside.

He crouched to touch the rough walls, relishing the coolness against his palm. A swath of emerald moss, plush and springy, covered the ground. Tendrils of ivy curled at his feet. In the distance, there was a willow tree.

He could scarcely make out the initials etched faintly into the wood.

L.B.

Lillian Beaumont's hidden refuge.

Olivia crouched beside him. More letters emerged below the L.B. etching, spelling a name—StormyCuddle—before the letters trailed off, obscured by debris.

"StormyCuddle? What kind of nickname is that for Lillian's secret love?"

Questions bounced between them. Was Stormy the writer of the letter?

"This is incredible," he said. Near the carved L.B. initials, he scraped broken vines rambling along the stones. "Someone has been here recently."

"Who?"

"I'm not sure."

"Anyone can walk here. This is a public forest."

"Feels like a whole different world, though, doesn't it?"

"Yes, but none of this solves the puzzle." Olivia flung the words out and blew out a breath. "We're still stuck without a clue about the mystery man's identity, let alone his apparent nickname."

"We're moving forward." Daniel resisted the urge to remind her they had found the gazebo, and it was a start. Her assumption that they were at the finish line rather than the starting gate meant she needed more encouragement.

When she opened her mouth, presumably to refute him, he slipped his arm around her shoulders, and gave her a bolstering squeeze.

Her eyes, usually filled with determination, shimmered with vulnerability.

"Ollie, we suspect this gazebo was special to Lillian," he began. "We may not have all the answers, but we've come this far. I promise we'll figure it out."

Her delicate eyebrows creased. "We'll?"

"Yes. You and me." His thumb traced circles on her shoulder. "Think of this discovery as expanding our knowledge. If it falls through, we can always give Lillian the letter so she can read the contents and decide for herself."

"I don't want to upset her until I know the truth about the sender."

"No one in this town would ever hurt her. Or you." Daniel hoped his confidence offered reassurance, prying Olivia loose from her worries. "More clues are bound to surface if we stay patient and keep digging."

Her lips parted, but instead of an argument, an uncertain smile formed.

His heart ached to erase her uncertainty.

"We'll sort this out," he assured.

As her smile expanded, he kept her close. The quiet sounds of the woods folded around them—the birds twittering in the treetops, the noiseless wind vibrating the budding spring leaves.

Without warning, a kaleidoscope of memories overwhelmed him.

Reading mysteries together in the town park. Private scribbles tucked into worn library books. Awkward teenagers tentatively bridging a gap toward something more, until high school graduation tore it all apart, and he left for college.

It was all his fault. He should've stayed.

Shaking off bittersweet nostalgia, he focused on the diary. This town's history bound everyone together.

What happened between Lillian and her clandestine boyfriend? Did she find her happily ever after? Or did obligations eventually separate them too?

His gaze wandered to the nickname carved into the wood. The incomplete riddle was intriguing. Perhaps Lillian's admirer still lived in Sweetwater Springs.

Olivia's phone chirped, jolting them back to the present.

"It's near time for my interview with Walter and Harriet McAllister." She checked her watch. "They were in their teens when they attended high school with Lillian. Maybe they'll share insights about her secret romance."

"Did you tell them about the letter?"

"No. I wanted to speak with them first."

Daniel nodded. "Married for over 50 years—they must have some interesting stories."

"I'm hoping they do. Lots and lots of them."

As they emerged from the woods, the birds fell eerily silent. When a twig snapped in the thicket behind them, his muscles seized.

"We should hurry," he said, picking up their pace toward town.

As they walked hand in hand, he stole a sideways glance at Olivia. Her flawless complexion glowed, accentuating her classically beautiful bone structure and large, expressive eyes.

She exuded an air of confidence and capability. She always insisted on doing things by herself, displaying an independent spirit. However, there was a simmering vulnerability underneath. Confined by other people's expectations, she rarely voiced her dreams and downplayed her business successes.

His connection to her grew. They had always operated as a team, their minds in sync as they pieced together clues and formed theories.

He watched her, admiring the way she absently twirled a strand of her chestnut hair around her finger. His feelings had never truly faded—they had only grown stronger with time and distance.

Olivia glanced up at him, catching him staring. "Daniel." Her voice trembled. "I—"

He leaned in, his kiss sweet and full of promise. His heart pained, contemplating her being dismissed as a "predictable homebody" when he saw her courage and ambition so clearly. If only she could see herself from his perspective.

When the kiss ended, Olivia beamed up at him, lighting up those mesmerizing brown eyes. "What are you thinking?" she asked.

He gave her hand a squeeze. "Merely admiring the view." If only she knew how he was realizing how desperately he still loved her after all these years apart. How leaving Sweetwater Springs—and her—had shattered him completely for a while, although he'd vowed to see the world before settling down.

She stifled an exhale. "Maybe the McAllister's can provide insights into Lillian's past. I said that already. Right?"

"Right." He nodded, reminded again of her boundless empathy and care for others. Under her intrepid pursuit was a desire to protect Lillian. Her dedication made his heart swell with pride and affection. She exuded confidence and grace, a true businesswoman through and through.

The woods gave way to the town park, where they'd spent uncountable afternoons beneath the shade of a giant oak tree, reading thrilling explorations, lost in imaginary worlds.

"Remember when we tried to find a buried chest of gold, we were convinced the town founder left it behind?"

She laughed. "Instead, we dug up Mrs. Conklin's flower bed."

He grinned, warmed by the musical sound of her laughter.

He needed no treasure chest—simply being together had been magical enough. If he could make her laugh, explore by her side, and share those quiet, hidden moments, he was the luckiest guy in Sweetwater Springs. When ambitions and dreams threatened to tear them apart, this remained his most precious truth.

"We'll figure everything out together," he assured.

And I'm not going anywhere, he silently promised.

As they made their way back to town, she paused, turning to face him.

"Something doesn't add up," she said. "If Lillian's relationship was so secret, why would she risk meeting the man she loved in a public place like the gazebo?"

"Definitely a bold move, especially for someone in her position."

"And the way the diary ends so abruptly, without explanation …What if something happened to her? What if her relationship put her in danger?"

Daniel rested a comforting hand on her shoulder. "Anything is possible. In those days, a wealthy woman like Lillian being involved with someone her family disapproved of might have resulted in serious consequences."

"What if she didn't leave town voluntarily? What if someone forced her, or worse? What if …" She couldn't seem to bring herself to finish the sentence, though the implication hung heavy.

"If Lillian was in trouble, there may be clues we've overlooked," he reassured.

SOON, they arrived at the cottage of Mr. and Mrs. McAllister.

Olivia gave Daniel's hand a last squeeze before knocking at the bright-blue door. The door opened with a creak, revealing Mrs. McAllister's pale face.

Her pure-white hair was anchored by a decorative crystal hair clip.

"Olivia, my dear!" Her southern drawl lengthened her vowels. "And, butter my biscuit! Who is this handsome young man you've brought with you?"

Daniel held out his hand. "Daniel Whitfield, ma'am."

"You're little Daniel?" Mrs. McAllister's cardigan sweater and floor-length skirt were neatly pressed. "My, how you've grown! You must be over six feet tall."

"Six feet, two inches," he clarified.

The irresistible aroma of still warm oatmeal cookies

wafted from the kitchen, mixing with the scent of old magazines, several piles of newspaper, and Mr. McAllister's pipe tobacco.

A pot of both coffee and tea was set on a round end table in the living room.

They shed their coats while Mrs. McAllister poured steaming coffee in porcelain cups for each of them, along with a plate of oatmeal cookies.

They traded pleasantries and stood around a table, where Mr. McAllister waited on a floral couch, tufts of snowy-white hair haloing his shiny bald spot. The room soon filled with the heartening scent of burning wood in the crackling fireplace and the sound of low, shared laughter.

Daniel leaned over and shook hands with Mr. McAllister.

Though his wrinkled hands showed his age, Mr. McAllister's eyes crinkled cheerfully behind thick silver spectacles as he welcomed them. He set aside a photo album filled with aging polaroids.

"What brings you two here today?" he inquired, stirring his coffee. His pipe, resting on a nearby ashtray, carried a faint, musky aroma.

After Olivia took a seat in an armchair, Daniel sank into the downy, cushioned couch next to Mr. McAllister.

His gaze drifted to the photo album, and a black-and-white image of a youthful couple dancing. The woman's features were strikingly similar to Mrs. McAllister's. Beside it was a snapshot of a grinning young man wearing a football uniform.

"I was hoping you might remember something about Lillian Beaumont's romances," Olivia began.

"Ah, Lillian. That's the word. Romances. Plural." Mrs. McAllister bit her lip, then offered a shrug and a pinched smile as she took a seat. "I haven't seen her in some time, but I suppose she's as beautiful and classy as ever."

Despite her smile, Daniel detected a guardedness in her posture, as if bracing herself at the mention of Lillian's name.

He caught sight of the black-and-white wedding photo on the mantel. Joy had etched lasting laugh lines around the McAllister's' eyes, yet when Olivia mentioned Lillian, melancholy dimmed both of their expressions.

Mrs. McAllister's gaze came to rest on the antique knitting basket by her chair. Her husband inspected his coffee, his shoulders slumping. The weight of the past seemed to press on them.

While romance and steadfast commitment had sustained their marriage, perhaps Lillian signified lost chances and roads not taken. Perhaps her name carried an echo of what-could-have-been.

Olivia shot Daniel a cursory glance at the change in the couple's demeanor. As the fire crackled, he reached for her hand, hoping to convey wordless reassurance.

Mrs. McAllister slowly stirred a spoonful of honey into her tea, as if weighing her next words with caution. "In our youth, many areas of life were different in Sweetwater Springs. There were strict rules." She launched into a narrative of bygone days. "Back then, Lillian had all the boys in town wrapped around her little finger—my Walter included."

Mr. McAllister huffed and flushed red to the tips of his ears. "Now don't go spreading tales. Lillian was a friend. Merely an acquaintance."

Mrs. McAllister smiled, a far-away look in her eyes. "You fancied her, and you weren't the only one. All the boys were infatuated with her. However, her family had … higher aspirations than any of the locals. Gorgeous and refined, though also distant, in a way. It seemed like she was destined for something better than Sweetwater Springs could offer."

She exchanged a loaded glance with her husband.

"Yes, well." Mr. McAllister cleared his throat, his gaze

darting away from Daniel's curious stare. "Lillian played her cards close to her vest. We all did, back then."

"What do you mean?" Daniel asked.

Mrs. McAllister hesitated, her fingers twisting the delicate gold band on her left hand. "Oh, you know how it is in small towns. People talk, and sometimes … things get complicated. That's all in the past now. Lillian made her choices, and we made ours. That's the way life goes."

"As I've told you a hundred times, from the moment I first saw you at Sweetwater High, no one could compare to my Hattie," Mr. McAllister replied. "You're my snuggle muffin."

Daniel studied the couple with fresh insight. He visualized a young, bespectacled Walter pining after popular Lillian, while gentle wallflower Hattie admired him from afar.

Time had proven that the steadfast Hattie was the right match all along. Lillian's name signified innocent lost youth, but also deeper bonds discovered.

Daniel glimpsed the dim outline of a heart-shaped locket tucked beneath the collar of Mrs. McAllister's high-necked blouse, likely containing a youthful photo of the two from early days.

What other riddles from their background tied them to Lillian's past? Sweethearts since the age of seventeen, the devoted couple were genteel guardians of the town's stories. Their cottage brimmed with books and magazines—history keepers in their own right.

"I believe Lillian never married," Olivia said. "She left town for many years."

"Yes, her uncle was quite ill and resided in another state. Her parents sent Lillian to help care for him. He lived in a large city … Tampa, Florida, and they shipped her off." Mrs. McAllister plucked a cookie from the plate and took a considerable bite. "Though there was a boy who wasn't suitable, according to Lillian's family. They claimed he was trouble and would ruin her reputation. But she loved him, fiercely and completely."

"Lillian dated a lot of guys," Mr. McAllister said.

"Yes, but we all saw the change in Lillian with this one." Thoughtfully, Mrs. McAllister chewed her cookie. "She was radiant and reminded me of a flower in full bloom."

"We never knew his name," Mr. McAllister said.

"True, dear. Anyway, she graduated from high school in Florida, then attended college and decided to stay. She contributed thousands of dollars to the city's philanthropic projects before returning to Sweetwater Springs."

"Why did she move back after all these years?" Daniel asked. The cookies on the table next to him were warm and melt-in-your-mouth delicious, with hints of raisins and brown sugar. The coffee, smooth and bold, was a perfect accompaniment.

"I suppose she wanted to return to her roots," Mr. McAllister said. "We haven't seen her much, although we never moved in the same circles."

Olivia indulged in a generous sip of coffee before her hand reached for her purse. "I found her diary in the library's attic today, and she wrote about meeting a man—"

"Lillian's diary?" Mrs. McAllister's smile evaporated. Her spouse froze, nearly spilling his coffee. An uneasy tightness sizzled the air.

Olivia set down her cup. She surveyed Daniel, then the McAllister's. "Did … did I say something wrong?"

Mrs. McAllister glanced at her husband, as if seeking guidance.

"Lillian's past. It's complicated." He seemed to struggle to find the right words. "There are things we don't fully understand."

"She was a bit of a mystery, even to those who knew her

best. And when she left town so suddenly …" Mrs. McAllister trailed off, shaking her head. "If you're determined to uncover the truth, be careful. The answers you seek may come at a price."

"What kind of price?"

"Believe me, the woman you know now was a different person in her youth."

Daniel grappled with the implications that Lillian's past was far more complex than they had ever imagined.

CHAPTER 4

a noticeable hush enveloped the living room.

Olivia's eyes met Daniel's in a silent acknowledgement.

"I'm sorry. I didn't mean to upset you, Mrs. McAllister," Olivia said slowly. "I presumed you might recall details about the unknown man Lillian wrote about in her diary."

With a trembling hand, Mrs. McAllister smoothed her pearl-pinned hair. "It's not always wise to go digging up the past, dear."

Mr. McAllister avoided Olivia's eyes. "We appreciate the visit, but I'm afraid we can't discuss Lillian anymore."

Why were they so rattled? Olivia's thoughts skittered like fireflies darting through the night.

Daniel touched her wrist, a silent cue to leave.

As Olivia stood, she picked up her cup and plate, intending to place her dishes in the kitchen sink.

"I'll get that." Mrs. McAllister approached to stand beside her. "I have the rest of the afternoon to tidy the house."

"I don't mind. It'll only take—"

"I said I've got it." Mrs. McAllister clutched Olivia's arm.

A harsh tone Olivia hadn't expected had come out of Mrs. McAllister's mouth, as if a herd of horses had galloped into the room unannounced.

"What happened all those years ago?" Olivia sized up the look on Mrs. McAllister's expression.

The elderly woman appeared caught between a quandary and a tight spot. Her hands fluttered before she invited Olivia and Daniel to sit back down. She claimed the seat across from them.

Mr. McAllister stared down at his coffee cup, apparently examining the workmanship of the porcelain.

"Back then, Lillian's parents had arranged her marriage to the son of another prominent family in town," Mrs. McAllister began. "She defied them and fell in love with a boy beneath her station."

"Who was he?" Daniel asked.

"That's not for me to say." Her reply provided no answer, though it implied she knew who he was. "I was her friend. I covered for her once when she snuck off to meet him."

"Does he still live here?"

"I can't elaborate, dear."

As Olivia mulled over the words, understanding fused her speculations. "When I mentioned Lillian's romance, I hoped for some answers."

"Sadly, you brought up memories I worked hard to forget." Mrs. McAllister's eyes took on a faraway sheen. "When her parents discovered the affair, they were furious and shipped her off."

"For parts unknown?"

"For a while, yes, although we all found out, eventually. In those days, living several states away from Washington State was like living on the moon."

With a coffee cup in hand, Olivia absorbed Mrs. McAllister's statements.

"I had no idea all this would stir up such difficult memories for you." Olivia knew she should close the subject. Instead, she fished for more details. "How did you cope with losing Lillian? You mentioned she was a dear friend."

"That year was agonizing, because her parents wouldn't allow us to communicate anymore." Mrs. McAllister's voice dropped to a pained mutter. "Lillian gave up so much for him —her family, her social standing, the life she knew. Maybe no one else remembers, but I do."

"I remember," Mr. McAllister said.

She met her husband's gaze. "I know you do, dear. I speak for both of us when I say we can't bear to see Lillian hurt again over teenage mistakes. She has successfully reestablished a sense of home and belonging here, and she deserves to be happy."

"This isn't about old gossip," Olivia conceded. "You still care about her."

"Despite my initial jealousy over her popularity, she was a lovely and devoted friend. When she lost everything, I didn't do enough to help her. I've regretted my inactions all these years and have never gotten the nerve up to go to her and apologize." Mrs. McAllister took Olivia's hands in hers. They bore the aged grace of time. "Promise me you'll be discreet with whatever you learn. However much has changed, the past still haunts in ways we seldom expect."

Cryptic words that meant anything or nothing.

"This all leads back to Lillian's secret romance?" Olivia asked.

Mrs. McAllister withdrew her hands. "Forget that I mentioned the entire subject. Now run along, dears."

"Might your son have any knowledge?" Olivia inquired.

"James? My sweet son? Certainly not. He has his plate full running his business, and he's in the process of moving to a new location. He's a top-notch businessman."

"Thanks to us," Mr. McAllister chimed in. "We taught him the value of a solid work ethic."

"He learned from the best," Olivia replied.

She vividly recalled the days when James would lend a hand at his parents' stall in the bustling farmer's market. Surrounded by the aroma of homemade jams, jellies, and freshly picked produce, James learned the lessons of hard work and dedication. The days were long, and the tasks demanding, yet James remained ever vigilant, tirelessly scanning the crowd for potential sales.

Currently, James owned and operated *McAllister's Game Haven*, a board game café offering residents a diverse collection of games, as well as friendly competition and comradery. He was actively involved in the community and had never married. He and Olivia dated for a brief spell, but the relationship hadn't worked out.

Mrs. McAllister pushed back her chair and rose. An instant later, she ushered them to the foyer, leaving Olivia reeling with more questions than resolutions.

"Huh. That was about as clear as mud," Olivia muttered, kicking a pebble along the sidewalk, as the heavy door slammed behind them. "We're chasing our tails here. Every time we think we're getting closer to the truth, we hit another dead end."

"I admit I don't believe they were completely forthcoming. Welcome to the glamorous world of mystery-solving, Ollie. Evidently, it's not all dramatic revelations and eureka moments like in the movies."

Her lips twitched. "Oh, and here I thought you were going to be my dashing hero, swooping in with all the answers."

"Hey, I'm doing my best here! This is a far cry from the puzzles we used to solve as kids. The level of risk has been elevated, and the clues are more hidden."

Olivia's smile faded, and she worried her bottom lip between her teeth. "Do you think … do you think we're in over our heads? I mean, what if we're poking a hornet's nest that's better left undisturbed?"

"I know it's daunting, and I know there are risks involved. Still, we can't back down now."

She leaned into him, resting her head on his shoulder as they resumed walking. "You always knew how to make me feel better. Even when we were kids, you had a way of making everything less challenging."

"You've always been the brave one, Ollie." He pressed a kiss to the top of her head, his voice low and tender. "You inspire me to be better, but …"

"But?"

He puffed out a breath. "But on another note, I didn't appreciate Mrs. McAllister mentioning your old boyfriend."

She stared up at him. "That's not being better."

"It's on my mind."

"For what it's worth, I brought James McAllister up."

"Somehow, that's worse. Are you still interested in him?"

"James McAllister? You're kidding, right? I haven't dated him in forever and a day."

Daniel reached out for her hand. "Word is, he's still pining for you."

"Pining, huh? I don't believe it."

"I do." His tone carried an edge that barely masked his jealousy.

"Fortunately, I'm not pining for him." She jerked her hand away. "You can't be serious. James is an old friend, and that's it. Period. Our relationship ended badly. He was much more interested in his board games."

"I don't care in the least about your past relationship with James."

"Oh, really?" Exasperated, she made to stride off. "You'd

never know it." She glared at the ground, trying to decide if she should explain further.

He faced her, a noticeable slump to his shoulders.

Tears welled in her eyes. "You're super focused on a romantic connection that happened years after you were gone. Now you have the audacity to march back into my life after being gone for so long? What claim can you possibly have over me?"

He flinched, raked a hand through his hair, and caught her hand. "If you don't credit me with caring about you after I left, at least credit me with caring about you now."

Her face heated. She looked away, trying to decide if he was truly jealous, or if this was his way of offering an apology for all those years when they had the chance to be together.

"Am I forgiven?" Tenderly, his thumbs stroked her warm cheeks.

She had difficulty finding her voice and cleared her throat. "I guess so." Although she wasn't sure exactly what he was apologizing for.

"You deserve so much better than me, Ollie. I was stupid for letting you go, but I swear I'll spend forever making it up to you."

He brought her close, within arm's reach, and kissed her, his breath merging with hers. Her heart beat in uneven lurches when they moved apart, and the intimate spell was broken.

As they walked through the town park, Olivia reflected on how much Sweetwater Springs had shaped her life. Every corner held a memory, every building a story. She had grown up here. She believed that she knew all there was to know about her beloved hometown.

But now, as they investigated Lillian's past, Olivia questioned herself. The secrets they were uncovering, the hidden truths lurking beneath the surface of the town's history, were like seeing Sweetwater Springs through new eyes.

She glanced at Daniel, wondering if he experienced the same sense of unease, the same realization that the place they'd always called home might not be quite what it seemed. How many other secrets lay buried in the past, waiting to be discovered? And what would it mean for their future, for the life Olivia had built here?

As they passed an ancient oak tree where they had spent numerous afternoons, a pang of nostalgia mixed with her uncertainty. Sweetwater Springs was her constant, her anchor in a world full of change. Despite the mystery unfolding, she struggled to let go of a suspicion that what she had previously assumed was on the verge of being turned upside down.

They continued, hand in hand, through the town square.

Olivia was incapable of ignoring the electricity that crackled between them. The years they'd spent apart had only intensified their connection, the unspoken understanding that had drawn them together since childhood. He had always been her rock.

He paused and turned to her. "When I went away, I never stopped thinking about you, wondering what you were doing, if you were happy."

"What prompted that?"

"Just something I needed to say."

"I'm happy now. With you, I'm exactly where I was meant to be."

His arms wrapped around her waist. "Whatever happens, we're in this together," he murmured, his breath tickling her ear.

He captured her lips in a searing kiss, and Olivia was certain that he meant every word. They had a long way to go, both in solving the mystery and in navigating their own relationship. Nonetheless, in this perfect moment, everything was right in the world.

They continued to walk, and she broached a thought. "We don't have definitive proof, but I found it strange when Theodore started humming, *I Love You More Today Than Yesterday* after I mentioned the letter to him. What connection could our local poet possibly have with Lillian?"

"You mentioned that Emma was curiously invested in Lillian's letter. And Theodore pops into your shop daily. Maybe he provided tips to the letter writer about people and places that were special to Lillian in her youth. Worth looking into, at least as a potential lead."

"Hmm." Olivia turned the idea over in her mind. "And he is rather eccentric. Who knows what ideas are brewing beneath all that senior charm?"

Perhaps Theodore had insider knowledge about the admirer's identity. A further investigation might uncover clues to tie the letter back to its rightful author.

"The diary unearthed some painful recollections for the McAllister couple," Daniel said.

"Are they hiding something about Lillian's past? Is there a chance they are safeguarding her long-lost love?"

"You should've told them about the letter addressed to Lillian from the unidentified sender. It's possible they would've recognized the nickname, StormyCuddle."

"Mrs. McAllister was too upset for me to bring up anything else." With the torrent of questions swirling in her mind, Olivia suggested a change of scenery. "Let's stop at the café."

"*Pages and Aromas*? I'm still buzzing from all the caffeine I drank today."

"Well, I only had one cup of coffee. Besides, I'm starving."

"So am I."

"Again? You devoured at least a dozen of Mrs. McAllister's oatmeal cookies."

"And you ate only a couple." He winked at her. "It's your suggestion, but I insist on treating."

"Deal. You make more money than I do, anyway."

"How do you know?"

"You bought a house on Windsor Boulevard."

He laughed and grabbed her hand. Moments later, they sauntered into the busy café and took a seat.

The aroma of recently roasted coffee beans and the tempting sweetness of frosted pastries enveloped Olivia. The gentle clinking of cups and murmured conversations created a soothing backdrop, a momentary reprieve from the whirlwind of their investigation.

Sunlight flooded the expansive windows, illuminating the rustic wooden tables. The vivid artwork on the walls combined abstract strokes of vibrant reds and blues.

As they settled into a secluded corner booth, Olivia ran her fingers over the plush seat. The texture was soft and relaxing.

Daniel's voice was low as he picked up a menu and discussed it with her.

Olivia leaned in closer, her knee brushing against his beneath the table. The rest of the world seemed to fade away, leaving only the two of them, lost in the intimacy of the moment.

"Since you're treating ..." Smiling, Olivia ordered a sliced turkey sandwich stuffed into a cheese croissant, a green side salad, and a cup of bergamot tea. Daniel requested the same.

The inviting aroma of cinnamon, ginger, and spiced tea surrounded them. They traded viewpoints between bites, the lively whirr of activity creating normalcy to their peculiar day, grounding them in the present.

Olivia found his face far more compelling than the half-eaten croissant on her plate. His warm hazel eyes met hers, and she was lost in the intimacy of the moment.

His strong hands cradled his cup of tea, the steam rising in tendrils and curling around his forehead. The fragrance of bergamot and honey mingled with his woodsy scent, a heady combination that made her pulse quicken.

"You were better at solving puzzles than I was," he was saying.

Was he being genuine, or trying to flatter her?

She couldn't suppress her laugh. She recalled countless instances when his intellect outshone hers. The school projects, the late-night study sessions—he invariably grasped concepts quicker and more effortlessly. "Do you think I was born yesterday? You're the smart one."

"Nope. Purely the opposite. I always had confidence in you." His rough thumb stroked her knuckles, and she shivered at the tingle that traveled up her arm. "What else do you remember?"

"When we were kids, we read "Choose Your Adventure Series" in my grandfather's shop." They'd find a snug space, and flip through pages with the speed of a hummingbird's wings. "Who would've imagined that we'd be pursuing our own real-life whodunit as adults back here in Sweetwater Springs?"

"Some things are meant to be, Ollie."

She reached for her croissant, her fingers breaking off a piece. "Remember the night we found Mrs. Henderson's missing cat?"

"Oh, the cat in the storm drain? How could I forget?" He set down his fork after sampling his salad." We were twelve years old."

"We had just entered junior high school." A silent chuckle teased behind her reminiscing. "We followed a lead, heard rumors about strange noises near the drains. So, armed with flashlights, we decided to investigate."

"Yeah, it was late, and the town was super quiet. You said the square was like a giant puzzle, missing some of its pieces." He spooned a dash of sugar into his tea. "Then we reached the spot where the drain openings were located."

"That's when we heard faint meowing. We followed the sound, and there it was—Mrs. Henderson's cat, stuck in the drain."

"Poor thing must've been there for days. We tried to reach the cat, but the opening was limited."

"We called our parents, and they cheered, then scolded us for sneaking out late, plus it was a school night." Olivia stared at her plate, as if engaged in an intimate dialogue with her sandwich. She sighed and dashed a tear from her eyes before looking at him. "I miss them both so much."

"Me, too. Our beloved parents passed away too soon." He laced his fingers with hers. "Remember they contacted the town maintenance, who helped rescue the cat? Mrs. Henderson was overjoyed. Turns out, a few animals were getting stuck in those old storm drains."

Remember, remember, remember.

Their laughter mingled with quiet sadness. The café held a pause, acknowledging the shared ache of loss. His hand on hers spoke more than words, grounding them in a reality of a past that had shaped them.

"The relief on Mrs. Henderson's face made it all worthwhile." Olivia dipped a piece of buttery croissant into her tea, letting the fragrant liquid soak into the layers before taking a reflective nibble. "Those days were awesome."

"A story with a happy ending, Ollie. It started with a cat, a storm drain, and ended with a lot of relief." He went back to stirring his tea. "The town realized they needed to secure those drains. We unintentionally became community heroes."

"Yeah, from investigators to cat rescuers."

"If I get to be Watson to someone's Sherlock Holmes, I'm glad it's you." His gaze dropped briefly, remaining on her mouth before finding her eyes again. "Think we'll rival Benedict Cumberbatch one of these days?"

Olivia's laugh came out huskier than she expected. "Who's he?"

"He solves crimes in a small town, and we're giving the British actor a run for his money these days."

"We sure are." They both leaned across the table, and their lips met, erasing the café and all its noise. Surely, he heard her thudding heartbeat.

Kissing him felt both ingrained and exhilarating, a ballet her body intrinsically remembered while rediscovering at the same time. His eyes were a fascinating blend of colors— shades of brown, green, and hints of gold.

When they broke apart, Daniel cradled her hands in his larger ones.

"What are we getting ourselves into?" she asked. "The more we learn about Lillian, the more I fear we're opening a can of worms that shouldn't be opened."

"We can't walk away now. Lillian's story feels important. It's meant to be told."

She sighed, knowing he was right. Still, the doubts lingered, nibbling at the edges of her resolve. What if the truth they uncovered was too painful, too devastating?

She pondered the enigmatic warnings from the McAllister's, contemplating the indications of hidden secrets and scandals lurking beneath the surface of Sweetwater Springs' genteel facade. Part of her wanted to turn back, to retreat into the comfortable familiarity of her everyday life and forget all about Lillian's past.

Another part of her—the part that had always been drawn to puzzles and mysteries—refused to let it go.

"I'm scared," she said. "Scared of what we might find, of how it might change everything."

"I'm scared too." He kept her hands in his, caressing her fingers. "But we'll face it together, just you and me, like old times."

Olivia gained strength from his presence, his unwavering support.

"Okay," she said, taking a breath. "Let's keep going."

"Is there anything else besides the McAllister visit upsetting you?"

"What makes you ask?"

"The way you're staring blankly out the window instead of at me."

She withdrew her hands and took another bite of the croissant. "Oh, the usual cocktail of Lillian's secret love, sprinkled with a dash of fedora-clad intrigue."

"Sounds intriguing." He laughed. "Hold on. Fedora?"

"It's probably nothing."

"Don't stop now."

She recounted the previous night when, after closing her bookshop, she spotted the limping man wearing the fedora.

Daniel tilted his head, a doubtful quirk on his lips. "Could you have imagined it?"

"I'm certain I didn't. Well, at least, I don't think I did." A hint of uncertainty delayed her voice, as if the encounter blurred the lines between reality and imagination, leaving her questioning the validity of her own perception.

"Then consider me lucky to be caught up in this whirlwind with you." Daniel captured her lips in another soft, prolonged kiss.

Her pulse beat a silent drum solo, and they existed in their own blissful bubble of companionship. If only she could stay with him like this forever, keeping the outside world at bay.

This was it—a hushed choreography of connection. Since his return to Sweetwater Springs, Daniel had reawakened long-buried feelings that both delighted and frightened her.

"From the second the letter arrived, my life has spun into a whirlwind," she said.

"I'm here for you. Now and always." His assurance wrapped around her heart like the security of a much-loved quilt. Gazing up through her lashes, she recognized the raw longing etched on his face because it matched her own. In that suspended moment, the only reality was each other.

Before they discussed the situation any further, the café's glass door banged open.

Dressed in a suit that struck a balance between timeless elegance and a touch of the unconventional, the man standing in the doorway held a magnetic presence. Dark, wavy hair framed a face concealed beneath the brim of a fedora. A cigarette dangled between two fingers. His exhale released coils of smoke into the air as he scanned the café.

Alarm swelled in her chest. She tried to stand, to move, but her steps hit a pause button.

"It's him!" she shouted, willing herself to shoot to her feet.

"Who?"

"The man in the fedora. The man from last night. He's real."

As Daniel pushed back his chair and whirled, the man seemed to evaporate, leaving an eerie trail of uncertainty.

A freeze in her movements framed the seconds.

"Did you see him?" she asked.

"No."

"He was there, clear as day. He was tall and wore a long black overcoat." She snapped her attention to the door, then reached for her coat. "How could you have missed him?"

Daniel offered a curt nod as she jostled past him. "I guess I didn't turn around quick enough."

Frustration pricked at her. "You guess? Well, I guess I'm the designated detective for today. We should go after him. He might have the answers we need."

"Okay, but let's be careful. We don't know who he is or what he's after."

Her mind raced as she tried to piece together what had happened. Or rather, what hadn't happened.

Had she imagined the man?

CHAPTER 5

"*I* saw him," a woman, her salt and pepper hair catching the sunlight, chimed from an adjacent table. Her voice carried a blend of nosiness and mischief. She, along with a group of women, had been sharing tales over coffee. "He's a newcomer, and we're all speculating about him."

"Who's we?" Daniel asked.

"Everyone in town. The name's Edith, by the way. Edith Montgomery. I've lived here my whole life, and I've seen my fair share of secrets. I couldn't help hearing you two while you talked."

"Can you tell us anything about this man, Edith?" Olivia paused and pulled up a chair.

Edith took a sip of her coffee, apparently savoring the moment. "Though I have a hunch, I can't say for certain if he is connected to the old Whispering Woods estate. You know, the place nobody has used for years?"

There was that word again. Whispering, although Olivia wasn't familiar with the estate.

"What makes you think that, Edith?" she asked.

The woman smiled, clearly enjoying the attention. "Call it a feeling. The estate has a bit of a scandalous history. Supposedly, the original owner named Nathaniel Ashcroft, a successful investor before he faced financial ruin, had a secret love affair with a local girl. A girl from a wealthy and prominent family, if you know what I mean."

"Do you think this man in the fedora is connected to the story?" Olivia asked.

Edith shrugged. "Like I said, it's only a hunch. If you're looking for answers about Lillian Beaumont's past, I'd start by digging into the history of Whispering Woods. There might be more to that old estate than meets the eye."

The woman indicated a group of retirees. "Every Sunday afternoon, we're here. It's half price day for seniors, and the retirement home shuttles us back and forth."

Several women shared observations.

"We have lots of theories," Edith said as Daniel tossed some bills on the table. "You know where to find us."

"Sure thing." Olivia acknowledged as she stood, darted between tables, and stepped outside.

"I can't believe you didn't see the fedora guy," she muttered to Daniel as he walked beside her. "He was right there. Directly in front of us."

"This again? You were facing the doorway. I was turned the other way, remember?" He pushed a hand through his hair. "I'm sorry, Ollie, but I missed him. Honestly, I'm taking this as seriously as you are."

"Are you? Sometimes it seems like you're just along for the ride, as if you're not totally invested in finding out the truth."

"That's not true. I care about this mystery, about Lillian, about … about you. More than anything in this world."

She searched his face, looking for any sign of insincerity, though all she found was a deep, unwavering devotion.

He pulled her close, his forehead resting against hers. "I'm beside you, every step of the way."

She closed her eyes and allowed his authenticity to wash over her. The soft cadence of his words, his powerful embrace, and the earnestness in his voice instilled an assurance of safety and belonging.

No matter the twists and turns, they'd weather the storm together. Because that's what love was—facing the unknown, hand in hand, and never letting go. And she was truly in love with him.

Their conversation circled back to the McAllister couple and their ambiguous warnings, plus the stealthy man in the fedora. And the new possibility—a man named Nathaniel.

"I keep thinking about what Mrs. McAllister said," Olivia mused. "What do you think she meant?"

"I'm not sure. Although it's clear, we need to be careful."

Olivia nodded, recalling the enigmatic note on the back of Lillian's black-and-white photograph in her diary.

"Secrets can be deadly," she murmured, more to herself than to Daniel.

"What? What did you just say?"

"I forgot to tell you. When I was looking through Lillian's diary, I discovered a vintage snapshot wedged between the pages," Olivia said. "On the back, someone wrote, 'Secrets have consequences' in red ink.

"What type of consequences? Could it tie into the mysterious man in the fedora, who seems to watch our every move?"

"Maybe. Or maybe Lillian wrote it. What does it mean for our investigation?"

"Okay, we need to talk to Lillian." His voice lowered. "She needs to be aware of what we've discovered, and she might have answers for us. But Ollie, promise me you'll be careful when I'm not around."

"I am."

"Are you? You operate your bookshop all alone."

As they walked hand in hand through the streets of Sweetwater Springs, the shadows seemed to lengthen and twist.

Lost in conversation, she didn't notice the lone figure walking toward them until she looked up. Stiffening, she grabbed Daniel's arm. As the figure drew closer, a quiet exhale of relief tripped out. It was only Theodore, his blue eyes twinkling behind round spectacles.

"Olivia! Daniel! Lovely to see you both!" Theodore sported a baggy brown corduroy jacket, complete with a pocket square. His white hair was combed neatly to the side. "I'm headed out for my nightly constitutional. Care to join a seasoned citizen?"

Seasoned. Cute.

Daniel glanced at Olivia. "We can't. We were discussing—"

"The stranger. I overheard your conversation." Nora appeared beside Theodore, smoothing her tweed skirt, a lightweight blazer draped over her shoulders. "I finished work early. The odd fellow lurking about—the one in the sleek suit and fedora. Yesterday, I spotted him leaving the room where important records are stored."

Daniel shook his head, dazed. He looked as if someone had thrown a water balloon at him and missed. "Why would he be there?"

Nora pushed her slipping glasses up her nose. "I'm sure he had his reasons."

If this stranger had accessed any records, what was he looking for? And did his actions connect to Lillian? Somewhere out there, perhaps, he was a silent guardian of the past, waiting to strike.

"He was at *Pages and Aromas* a few minutes ago." Olivia

looked around. Did he get swallowed up in the crowd of pedestrians who were out for a Sunday stroll? Or was he skulking out of sight around the corner?

With a casual flip of her hair, Nora averted her gaze. "Theodore and I were discussing him."

Daniel eyeballed Theodore. "You saw him, too?"

"Yes. Yesterday, and only for an instant." Theodore chuckled. "Certainly, a touch unconventional."

Olivia's conviction intensified. Did this man's link to Lillian's past hold true, or did his presence conceal an unexpected turn in the road? If both Theodore and Nora and the senior citizens had seen the stranger, then others likely had, too.

"What do you make of him, Theodore?" Olivia pressed, hoping to glean the poet's impression.

Theodore fiddled with his bowtie, ensuring it sat perfectly. "I confess, the man intrigues me. He arrived the same day as the mysterious letter appeared. Or at least, that's when everyone first saw him. And with a cigarette constantly in his grip—"

"Do you think he penned the letter to Lillian?" Olivia asked.

"Why not?" Theodore's eyes gleamed, suggesting a lifetime of wisdom. "Why, imagine! A silent admirer returns after years apart to declare himself to Lillian at last."

While Theodore waxed poetic about everlasting romance, Daniel caught Olivia's hand, interlacing their fingers. Again, she felt their own powerful connection. If this stranger had traveled miles to reunite with his long-lost love, then her relationship with Daniel buzzed with a quiet, newfound hope.

Nora coughed indiscreetly, breaking the moment. "As romantic as it sounds, let's consider the matter of the fedora guy settled."

Settled?

A shiver tiptoed along Olivia's back. An unwelcome and questioning partner. The man provoked more intrigue than fear, though Nora had a point. Perhaps there was nothing else to it. Yet Olivia felt unseen eyes trained on their progress.

"Have you heard of a man named Nathaniel Ashcroft?" she asked Theodore.

"Unfortunately, yes. He was an older guy, rich, and he liked to hang out with the younger crowd. That was all of us —me and my classmates. Nathaniel preferred dating high school girls, although it was unseemly. He lost everything and moved out of town. Good riddance to him."

In the quiet recesses of her mind, Olivia entertained the idea of Nathaniel and Lillian's romantic history but opted to keep the inquiry tucked away unsaid.

Her gaze snagged on a flicker of motion. Half-obscured in the doorway of the library stood the stranger. His dark, piercing eyes met hers for a split second before he disappeared into the alley.

She clutched Daniel's arm with both hands. "Did you see him?"

"Who?" Daniel followed her gaze and blinked.

"The guy in the fedora. Why do you always miss him?"

She let go and cinched her wool coat tighter, warding against the stubborn nip in the air. Strands of hair escaped her ponytail, tickling her neck like whispers in the wind.

Scanning the looming mountain backdrop, she expected to see storm clouds gathering. However, only shopkeepers swept porches, while two giggling toddlers clutched their ice cream cones, dripping trails marking their meandering route along the sidewalk.

Theodore reached into his pocket and yanked out a carved cedar box. "Care for a glimpse into the past?"

"A journey into history?" Daniel asked. "Now?"

"Why not? Window shopping in a bygone era while we walk. Nothing can compare. Old stories have a way of breathing life into the present." Theodore opened the box to unveil a collection of antique postcards, each bearing a unique snapshot of the town. The faded images captured moments suspended in time. Slid among the postcards was a bundle of meticulously tied parchment, each sheet covered with handwritten poems. "Poetry, my friends, is the true soul of life."

He selected a postcard showcasing a vintage scene— cobblestone streets with Model T Fords parked beside the curb. As they continued, he recited verses, echoing the sentiments of the postcard scenes.

The four of us, Olivia reflected, marching along as if we were bound for Oz. Perhaps the ordinary might unveil the extraordinary, or, at the very least, an answer.

"In each locale, a tale unfurled, a poetic symphony that spanned the world," Theodore went on. "With every step, my words took flight, turning a simple promenade into a lyrical delight."

"All well and good, Theodore, and your poems are clever. But where, exactly, are we headed?" Nora asked.

Oz, Olivia thought. She bent the collar of her jacket higher, and then her fingers found Daniel's.

He lowered his head, his breath skimming her hair. "Are you shivering?"

"It's cold."

"And you're nervous."

"Yes, a littlc."

"Stop worrying. I'm here for you."

She offered a brave smile. Nonetheless, questions nagged. What did the stranger want? Why did he keep appearing? And most importantly, was he the man who wrote the letter?

"He couldn't have gone far," she said. "We can try to find him."

Nora hesitated. "You all go on. After my shift at the library, I'm exhausted."

"Nonsense." Theodore tucked the box of postcards back in his pocket. "Come. I insist." He indicated that he and Nora would walk ahead. "Let's speed up before the guy gets away from us."

Further on, the alley narrowed. Cement walls were covered in years of graffiti scratches and old bubblegum. The area desperately begged for a thorough cleaning and a fresh coat of paint.

Olivia groped her way. A crumpled flyer stirred in a slight breeze.

As they ventured deeper into the alley, the air grew thick with the pungent odor of decay and neglect. The narrow passage was a world away from the quaint charm of Sweetwater Springs' main street, a forgotten corner where the town's secrets seemed to fester and grow.

Olivia's footsteps echoed on the damp pavement, mingling with the distant drip of a leaky pipe and the skittering of unseen creatures in the shadows. The walls loomed on either side, their once-vibrant brick mottled with grime and graffiti, a patchwork of faded colors and illegible scrawls.

A chill wind whipped through the alley, carrying with it the acrid tang of cigarette smoke and the sickly sweet stench of rotting garbage. Olivia shivered as she navigated the uneven terrain, her shoes crunching on scattered litter and broken glass.

Overhead, a sliver of gray sky peeked through the gap between the buildings, casting a wan, diffuse light. The metal stairs of the rusty fire escapes creaked and groaned in the breeze.

As they pressed on, the alley narrowed, the walls drawing closer as Olivia's senses went on high alert.

She scanned the gloom for any sign of the mysterious man in the fedora.

Beside her, Daniel acted as a source of support, his hand unwavering on the small of her back. She detected the tension in his body, the coiled readiness of a man prepared for anything. Together, they forged ahead, their footsteps a determined rhythm against the eerie stillness.

"No sight of him yet," Daniel muttered.

Nora slowed, then stepped behind them.

"Don't dawdle!" Theodore sang out at the end of the alley.

With Daniel's steadying presence, Olivia ventured past stacks of wooden crates and garbage bins.

Dimness sprawled ahead, concealing the stranger's retreat. Where was he headed? And what awaited them around the next bend?

As they exited, Theodore veered off, and Olivia, Daniel, and Nora continued walking.

CHAPTER 6

*O*livia searched for any movement. Had the limping stranger come this way? She could've sworn he had. Or had he somehow given them the slip?

Ahead stood a modest courtyard with a bubbling fountain at its center, and a clock tower. Empty shops, some with second-story apartments, backed onto the space. Flower boxes dotted windowsills bursting with spring blossoms, filling the air with a sweet scent. Cascading fuchsia rhododendrons spilled over the edges, their velvety petals brushing against the rough stone, while daffodils remained tall in a golden salute to the sun. Meanwhile, a tabby cat dozed on a precariously narrow window ledge, its soft fur ruffling in the breeze.

Theodore ambled to the fountain, squinting into its clear waters. "No lurking figures here. Only a little oasis tucked away from the world."

"Quite lovely," Nora agreed. "However, our trail has gone cold, so I'm heading home."

Olivia stopped short. A fountain. Lillian had etched vivid

descriptions of this very fountain in her cherished diary. It was where she often met her mysterious guy.

Her gaze stayed on the intricate details—the meticulously sculpted figures suspended in their own moments.

"This is the place Lillian described, isn't it?" Daniel asked. "I've never been back here."

"Neither have I. It's like stepping into the pages of her diary." Olivia circled the fountain, her fingers trailing across the smooth, cool stone, relishing the fine mist of water on her skin.

Connect the dots, she told herself. Connect the dots.

A door flew open, and out limped a slender, sharp-featured man with a beaked nose and wearing a fedora. Recognition dawned, along with unease.

"That's him!" Olivia began to follow him, but Nora held up a hand.

The man bypassed Olivia and limped straight to Nora. He pulled off his fedora and shook a mass of wavy, dark hair, like a wolverine shaking droplets from its fur.

After furtive, hushed, and uneasy murmurs, Nora pocketed an envelope he passed to her before returning to the door of his presumed apartment.

Olivia felt as if an icy deluge of water had been thrown over her, requiring her utmost focus to be sure her mouth hadn't dropped.

Daniel appraised Nora; a silent question etched on his face. "What was that about?" he asked.

"Umm, merely an old family friend passing through town." Nora glanced around the square as her laughter escaped too forcefully.

"I thought you didn't know the guy." Olivia's razor-sharp stare was glued to Nora. "Now he's a family friend?"

"Ah." A flush crept up Nora's neck. "I … must've been

mistaken. When I got a closer look, I recognized him as a long-time friend from my mother's family."

Her attempt to brush off the incident fell woefully short.

"What's his name?"

"Victor Steele."

"Where does he live?"

"Somewhere out of town. Why?" Nora fairly growled, her voice cutting through the air.

"An old family friend who slips you envelopes near back alleys? Curious." The lines around Theodore's eyes deepened. "Come now, Nora. Do you honestly expect us to believe you?"

"Odd doesn't begin to describe what just happened." Daniel's hand made a quizzical motion as he spoke. "What's going on?"

What was going on, indeed? A thousand frozen pinpricks covered Olivia's forearms with an ominous chill. First, Nora was wary, and now she was friendly with the fedora guy?

Nora lifted her chin, a defiant glint in her eyes. "You all have overactive imaginations. Sweetwater Springs is a sleepy town, and there are no mysteries or intrigues here. Can't two old friends acknowledge each other?" She pivoted; her steps purposeful, as she vanished into the alley.

Perhaps he was a distant relative who had gotten mixed up in something illegal. Nora was the loyal type who protected family members, even if it meant keeping mum.

Olivia mentally flagged the need for a private chat with Nora, determined to untangle the threads of this strange encounter. This man might hold the missing pieces. In the meantime, Nora was committed to keeping her role shrouded in mystery.

James McAllister emerged from a shop, interrupting their speculation. Despite being in his mid-40s, he wore the years lightly. His hair, a contrast between auburn and darker tones, brought a touch of maturity to his overall appearance.

"Olivia! Is that you?"

His voice stopped her cold.

"James!" Olivia's arms crossed loosely over her chest, her heart sinking as the tall man approached her. "What on earth are you doing here?"

"I'm relocating my business to this part of town." His steely, blue-eyed gaze sparkled. "I didn't expect to run into you like this."

"Your parents mentioned you were moving. What happened to your old location?"

"Maintenance has never been my strong suit. If things need updating, it's my cue to move on. Besides, this is an up-and-coming area that's been neglected for years. Plus, the rent is cheaper."

Olivia shifted under his prolonged stare.

"How's everything?" He leaned against a doorframe and produced a set of keys.

She looked away, tempted to ask, 'Do I have something on my face?' Aloud, she said, "Good. How's business for *McAllister's Game Haven* these days?"

"Same old. As I said, it was time for a change. Roll dice and share laughs over a board game." James offered a nonchalant lift of his shoulders, oblivious to her cues to stop staring.

"Is there another way to get to your place besides the alley?" Olivia gestured behind her. "We came through there, and it might hurt your business."

"The main street in town leads right to it."

She nodded. "Good to know."

"You always had exceptional foresight for displays and decor." He closed the distance between them with a

75

measured stride. "If you're free the next few days, I'd appreciate your input on my new place."

Daniel moved to her side, stealing a protective arm around her shoulders.

James' gaze slid to Daniel, and his smile faltered. "Who's this guy?"

Daniel extended his hand, his expression guarded. "Daniel Whitfield. Olivia and I are good friends."

"Good friends, huh?" James shook Daniel's hand. "Funny, she never mentioned you before."

"We grew up together. You were a few years older, so you probably don't remember him." Olivia spoke quickly, eager to diffuse the situation. "He moved away after high school and has recently returned."

James nodded, but his eyes remained fixed on Daniel. "And what brings you back after all this time? Business or pleasure?"

"A little of both," Daniel replied, his tone even. "I'm working at the historical society, but I'm also here to reconnect with old friends … and hope to make some new discoveries along the way."

Olivia's pulse quickened at the hidden meaning behind his words. She realized he was referring to their investigation into Lillian's past, although she couldn't dismiss the inkling that his statement hinted at something more personal.

James, oblivious to the subtext, clapped Daniel on the shoulder. "Good luck with that, buddy. And Olivia …" He turned to her. "I've missed you."

She swallowed; her throat was dry. "Thanks. Sorry, but we really should be going."

"By the way, James, Olivia is busy doing research at the library," Daniel said, adding a decided sharpness to his tone.

"Plus, with her full-time business, I doubt she'll have time for you."

"What kind of research?" James' gaze bounced between Olivia and Daniel. It didn't take much to register Daniel's presence and body language, and James finally got the cue and stepped back.

"A letter addressed to Lillian Beaumont arrived at my bookshop on Saturday," Olivia said. "We're trying to find out who sent it because there is no return name on the envelope. We suspect a man she dated many years ago. Some guy wearing a fedora sailed into town, and we thought it might be him."

James gave a deliberate, unhurried nod.

"Do you know him?" Daniel asked.

"A fedora? I've seen him once or twice." James' gaze darted around the square. "Does he have a name?"

"According to Nora Winters, his name is Victor Steele." Olivia caught a glimpse of an elderly gentleman sitting on a bench, feeding pigeons. "What if we ask people who live around here?"

James shrugged. "Can't hurt."

She paused, wedged in a moment of uncertainty. "I suspected Victor of writing the letter to Lillian, but after seeing him closely, I realize he's too young. Perhaps Victor is related to Lillian's guy in some other way."

"Maybe Victor Steele is Lillian's love child," James said.

"You're referring to a secret baby? Don't be ridiculous." Olivia's immediate reaction was a dismissive shake of her head. "Lillian is a well-respected and prestigious citizen. Nothing like that could've ever occurred."

Still, according to Mrs. McAllister, Lillian had left town before she graduated from high school, and she had dated several men in town.

"My parents mention Lillian often, especially when they reminisce." James lifted the keys in his hand. "Anyway, it's always a pleasure to see you, Olivia. If you and Daniel get a chance to stop by my new shop, it's opening soon, and my offer still stands."

The eager note in his voice had diminished considerably.

Theodore reentered the courtyard, having come from a walk between the shops. "Oh, James! You're precisely the person I was hoping to run into."

James paused his exit and turned. "What's up?"

"We had a run-in with an enigmatic gentleman in a fedora. Slender build, beaked nose, a prominent limp. I don't suppose you've seen him?"

"Only for a brief moment." His eyes flickered to Olivia. "Why don't you ask Delilah Fitzwater to help you?"

Initially startled, Olivia widened her eyes without blinking. "The ukulele player?"

"For years, she played the role of the town's matchmaker," James replied. "In fact, Delilah was instrumental in bringing my parents together."

"Is it possible she might be able to identify who Lillian dated when she was a teen?"

"Who knows? She might've been the cupid."

"Delilah "Harmony" Fitzwater," Daniel stated. "We saw her the other day."

The official free spirit of Sweetwater Springs, Delilah, had an oversized personality and a zest for life.

"Harmony is her middle name?" Olivia inquired.

"Yes. She earned the nickname because of the tunes she plays on the ukulele," James replied. "She once told my parents that every time two potential partners meet, it's like a love song waiting to be composed."

"I never knew much about her," Olivia said. "Thank you, James."

"Always happy to help, especially if it means I get to see you—I mean, happy to help solve your mystery." He flushed slightly and headed off, keys jangling in his fist.

As he walked away, Olivia let out a breath she hadn't realized she'd been holding. She pivoted and faced Daniel. "I'm sorry. James and I ... we're history."

"Right. So, you've said."

A pause punctuated Olivia's steps as she and Daniel veered toward the town, heading the opposite way from the alley. "In all this excitement the past few days, I forgot to lock up a rare first edition book I purchased at a thrift store the other day. Can we swing by my bookshop?"

"Sure." Daniel's stride adjusted to their new destination. "What's the name of the book?"

"*Ephemeral Shadows*, a long-lost novel by the bestselling author Elara Whitewood."

"I never heard of it."

The book had become a sought-after gem among bibliophiles and collectors. Olivia had stumbled upon it at a tucked-away used goods store, hidden beneath layers of forgotten novels, and felt an immediate connection to its haunting narrative.

As they entered the back door of her shop a half hour later, Olivia groaned. One of the supports on the storage shelf had split, causing the entire structure to tilt dangerously. A few novels had slid off, and she gathered them into her arms before more tumbled free.

"What happened here?" Daniel asked.

Olivia transferred the novels to a table. "The old shelf finally gave out. Of all days!"

He crouched, inspecting the split wood support. "I can patch this up for you really quick, no problem."

"How? No store is open this late, and I don't have any tools."

"I stocked up at the 24-hour corner mart yesterday. I'll go to my house and get the supplies."

"Such a long walk?"

"Luckily, this is a walkable town. I'll be back in a jif."

Olivia smoothed out a loose curl. "That would be amazing, but only if it's not too much trouble."

"No trouble at all. Be right back."

Time passed before he returned, the low hum of a car engine announcing his arrival. As he reappeared, he carried an assortment of tools and a bundle of fresh lumber, the scent of cut wood hanging in the air.

"I drove back," he confessed with a sheepish grin. "To save time.

"I heard your car pull up."

She flashed back to their youth, a time when he showcased his knack for repairing things. He once had fixed the creaky back gate of her home with an improvised latch made from an old coat hanger. Another time, he'd crafted a makeshift birdhouse from scraps of wood, their shared laughter filling the air at the number of birds it attracted.

His was a skill that had charmed her then, and here it was, coming to her rescue once more.

Daniel set to work, his movements deliberate and efficient. The tools resonated through the room; the sound of repairs was underway. With adroit precision, he reinforced the weakened areas and secured the shelf.

"There, good as new." He brushed his hands together, leaving behind the residue of sawdust, and stepped back to admire his handiwork. The once-fragile shelf stood secure and resilient, a testament to his dedication to the task at hand.

"I can't thank you enough." Olivia graced him with a brilliant smile. "How can I repay you?"

"By being here. By being you." He kissed her, long and hard. "I'm happy to help you anytime, Ollie."

Her chest brimmed with affection, fueled by his heartening smile and untiring assistance. She was thankful his choices had led him back into her life at precisely the right moment.

CHAPTER 7

*T*he following day, the sun filtered through the trees as Olivia and Daniel strolled down Ripple Ridge Lane. They were on their way to interview Delilah Fitzwater, the unabashed free spirit who might hold the answer to unlocking the romantic mystery from Lillian's past.

"It's fortunate Emma is covering for you today," Daniel said to Olivia.

"She usually sells out of baked goods by the afternoon and was available. Besides, Monday is a quiet day. I thanked her profusely." Olivia turned to him. "What about you and your work?"

A wry smile creased the corner of his lips. "I keep my own schedule. Besides, one of my co-workers, Gus Stratton, has been around a long time and is one of the most conscientious guys I've ever known."

His thoughts circled around Olivia's friend Emma. He pictured the blond, remembering glimpses of her over the years. She'd taken over her late mother's bakery, but had a closed-off, solitary air as she whisked down the street and hardly ever made eye contact. Her only regular companion was Theodore.

Though she and Olivia were friends, Emma was ice-locked in mourning after her mother's death. He imagined her closing time without laughter ringing through her bakery, only sighs and clouds of recollections. She took sole responsibility for the family legacy rather than risk dependence or disappointment.

Perhaps she viewed Lillian's letter as a possible heart-break in some way, instead of a bridge to possibility, and that was why she'd acted suspiciously when Olivia had shown her the letter.

Daniel understood the hollowed-out emptiness, the instinct to protect one's expectations. Seeing Olivia's enthusiasm and openness reignited these past few days reminded him that the potential rewards of love justified the risks. He hoped Emma might remember that, too. He hoped she would trust sharing life with someone special.

The town's main square, located near the community grocery store, came into view.

A community bulletin board, a mishmash of local flyers, captured Daniel's attention. He didn't release Olivia's hand. His fingers curled around hers.

The board beckoned with a patchwork of announcements, and his gaze traveled over the faded flyers. He was drawn to a tattered poster announcing the annual potluck supper the last Sunday of April, celebrating the arrival of spring, with references to the occasion found in Lillian's diary.

Olivia swayed from one foot to the other as she eyed the poster. "Lillian's diary spilled the beans on all the town events, especially this one."

"Nothing changes here. I practically grew up with the potluck."

"Me, too. I can almost hear Lillian's words resounding through time."

"What if we bring a dish to the potluck? A nod to tradition?" Daniel asked. "Did she specify any food in particular?"

"Her parents often brought a salad from the community garden. It's the start of the planting period, but cool season vegetables are available. She mentioned that she loved my grandmother Rachel's deviled eggs."

"Do you still have the recipe?"

Olivia leaned into his side. "I can probably find it, although I haven't made deviled eggs in years."

"How hard is it to make deviled eggs?"

"My question exactly, although that question might be my famous last words. What about you? What are you bringing to the potluck supper?"

"Me?"

"Yes, you. Everyone brings food to share."

He hesitated, nodded. "I call it 'The Tower of Temptation.'"

"Which is what?"

He seemed to wrestle with a grin. "You'll have to wait and see."

She gestured toward the park, where a few flowering cherry trees stood, fifteen feet tall. The flowers ranged in color from soft pink to pure white.

"Years ago, the town initiated a custom where couples planted a tree as a symbol of love. When the man asked a woman to plant a tree with him, it was a proposal of marriage. Lillian's diary had a thing or two to say about that ceremony as well."

"I helped plant several trees when I was a kid. A practice as enduring as the hills themselves."

"For a town this size, the idea is quite romantic."

Their footsteps fell into a comfortable rhythm as they continued down the street.

He surveyed the timeless storefronts and enchanting facades in the buttery afternoon light, underscoring the town's simple beauty. Sweetwater Springs's heart beat steadily as it had for over a century—a testament to a community that bound family stories together through periods of prosperity and periods of loss.

Like a love letter resurfacing after decades.

As if generations longed to pass the flickering torch, reminding those still here that the past lived on as long as even one person remembered.

Gramophone songs once danced to in parlor twilight resounded down the same sturdy lanes. Echoes calling to them across the years—don't forget we were here once— vibrantly, fiercely here. Mystery letters sent by hearts no longer beating pressed into the hands of hearts, continuing to beat.

Piecing the fragments into a narrative. Into meaning.

Perhaps Sweetwater Springs' true heritage lay in these shared tales—what sustained, what connected, what romanced. Not facts relegated to record books, but the joys and aches, worn smooth as creek stones.

He glimpsed Olivia's profile. Her beauty was understated yet undeniable, with a small, thoughtful frown gracing her face.

"Speaking of traditions," he said, "Is Emma still interested in finding out the mystery of who sent Lillian's letter?"

"She isn't saying much, but when she isn't aware that I'm looking at her, she seems … wary. I can't explain it."

Soon, Delilah's Victorian-style house sprawled before them, painted a sunny yellow with lavender trim. The front porch was decorated with flowerpots exploding with pink and purple rhododendrons, accompanied by a haphazard collection of garden gnomes and red lawn chairs.

Daniel fought off the feeling that they were being watched. The neighborhood was quiet, but a gardener ducked out of sight behind some bushes further up the street.

An uneasy prickle worked its way up his spine.

Was the man eavesdropping? Or something more suspicious? Or were Daniel's nerves getting the better of him on this fading afternoon?

Nonetheless, he couldn't shake off the sensation that they weren't alone.

As they reached Delilah's front door, Olivia's gaze darted around the empty street. "Did you hear anything?"

"No." He swiveled, pivoting in response to the unease in her voice.

"Probably the wind," she murmured.

"Probably."

Did someone loiter close by without them noticing? Daniel was convinced that he detected cigarette smoke carried on the breeze, despite being aware that Delilah's home was cigarette free.

"You know what, Ollie?" he asked.

"What?"

"At first, I was curious about this mystery. But now?" He didn't wait for her to respond. "There's a personal investment on my part. It's more than mere curiosity."

"What changed?"

"In many respects, I relate to Lillian." Emotions tightened his throat. "I'm aware of what it's like to care about someone for years without being able to show it. Wondering 'what if' about a love you never got to have. This seems as though it's a second chance."

"What does?"

"Us."

How long had he yearned for Olivia, dating all the way back to when they were little more than friends? Pursuing this riddle felt like chasing the elusive thing called love.

"Is that what this all represents?" she asked. "A possibility for us?"

He lifted his shoulders. "This mystery has me hoping destiny intervenes if I keep faith."

"Faith is real. The verdict is still out on whether fate has a hand in all this." She studied him, and her eyes misted. "We better see what information Delilah has in store for us."

She led him up the stairway strewn with leaves and stumbled, grabbing the railing for support.

His arm shot out to steady her. "Are you all right?"

Yeah." Olivia moaned and rubbed her ankle. "Strange. It was almost like someone lashed out at my heel." She scrutinized the empty front yard. The bushes at the end of the property rustled in the wind but remained still otherwise.

Daniel followed her gaze. In a flash of movement, a figure darted across the dirt path.

"Did you see that?" she asked.

He squinted. His body went rigid, poised for action.

Was there a footprint? Had somebody darted behind the shrubbery?

No. Best to continue forward, he told himself. I can't let paranoia derail the investigation.

The sound of lively ukulele music blared through the open windows of Delilah's home.

"Please don't tell me she's practicing *Tiptoe Through the Tulips,*" he whispered.

Olivia giggled. "She's playing *Can't Help Falling in Love* by Elvis Presley."

"What song would you perform if you were a ukulele virtuoso?"

"A big *if* on both of those counts. I suppose I'd pick *Aloha*

Oe. Ukuleles always make me imagine Hawaii." Olivia laughed, then sobered. "Okay, this is it. Are you ready?"

"I'm prepared if you are."

Olivia raised her hand as if to knock at the front door, then lowered it. "We left abruptly after Nora's odd interaction with Victor, and I haven't had the chance to catch up with her. I wonder if Theodore managed to learn anything more?"

"Knowing Theodore, he probably tried."

She blew out a breath. "Well, no time like the present, then." She gave the door three loud knocks.

Daniel took a quick look at the neighboring houses. Was a curtain twitching in the window of the home across the street? He strained his ears, hearing nothing but the wind in the trees.

After an eternity, the door creaked open, and Delilah Fitzwater appeared.

The large woman looked much younger than her sixty-odd years. Her flowing silver hair was topped by a crown of daisies. Her flamboyant patchwork skirt nearly blinded Daniel as she ushered them inside.

"Welcome, welcome!" She smiled widely.

"We liked your music—your playing, I mean," Daniel replied.

"*I Can't Help Falling in Love?*" Delilah hummed the chorus of the song, curiously off-key. Despite being a musician, she either had no sense of pitch, or she was tone deaf.

"I'm boiling a pot of hibiscus tea, and there are shortbread cookies on the coffee table. You're welcome to help yourself." Delilah bustled them into a living room bursting with flower garlands. The shelves were crammed with books, musical instruments, and eclectic knickknacks, and the cloying scent of potpourri mingled with herbal tea.

"Thanks, I'd love a cookie," Olivia said.

"I'm good for now." Daniel's gaze roamed to the floral wallpaper in shades of rose, the LP records stacked haphazardly by a vintage phonograph. Apparently, Delilah approached life with a different perspective than he did. He preferred his belongings to be neat and organized.

As he dropped onto the sofa beside Olivia, brocade cushions released a faint lavender scent. Lacy doilies, resembling ornate snowflakes, trimmed every tabletop, and chintz armchairs sunk under decorative piles of embroidered pillows. A heavy pink and white patterned stoneware tea set decorated a credenza behind a wingback chair.

A stained glass hanging in a lead-paned window scattered rainbow prisms, and the dark wainscoting and cabinetry soaked in the colors on a vibrant afternoon. Creaky hardwood floors were barely visible under scattered clusters of rugs and tapestries in clashing colors and mismatched patterns.

Delilah occupied a chair opposite them.

"We're hoping you can help solve a decades-old mystery about a local woman," Daniel began. "Did you ever arrange any dates for Lillian Beaumont?"

"Ah, Miss Lillian! Such a lovely girl. I arranged a few, but no gentleman fueled the special chemistry she longed for. She was such a romantic." Delilah let out a thoughtful sigh. "Although there was this man, oh, what was his name? He swept into Sweetwater Springs and Lillian was smitten. He was merely a traveler passing through, and she was devastated when he moved on. I can practically envision his handsome face smiling down at Lillian in the gazebo."

"You saw them?" Daniel asked.

"I shouldn't have snooped, but I was the matchmaker, so I took it upon myself."

"You chaperoned?"

"I wouldn't call it that. Lillian never realized I was there."

"What did he look like?"

"Clouds covered the sky, and it was dark, but I recognized Lillian's profile from a distance. They met at night, you know."

"You said he was handsome."

"Knowing Lillian, he probably was. She was rather discerning. She didn't date just anyone, though by my count she dated most every eligible guy."

As Delilah shared hazy recollections, eagerness spread through Daniel's veins. Finally, a witness! He slid forward, elbows braced on his knees. Olivia mirrored him, her spine taut.

"I arranged numerous dates for her," Delilah went on. "The guys who wanted to go out with her multiplied at every turn. She was gorgeous."

Daniel attempted to steer the conversation back to the gazebo. "So, you definitely observed her and a man together there?"

He met Olivia's wide-eyed gaze and resisted grabbing her hands in excitement. "She saw them!" he mouthed.

She gave a thumbs-up and bent nearer, lemon-scented hair cascading over her shoulders. A breath-stealing whisper of attraction momentarily suspended him.

"Do you remember anything else about him?" Olivia prompted Delilah. "A given or family name?"

Delilah cocked her head. Her eyes held a keen interest that surpassed a mere narrowing. "It's possible that his first name was Nathaniel or Tobias, or maybe Cleo; I can't recall. And his last name … Heatherton or Leathery or Albatross." She labored over to a cluttered desk and rummaged through a stack of papers. "I must've written it down somewhere."

Daniel's hands involuntarily reached for his chest. "You still have notes after several decades?"

"Of course. Why not?"

The teakettle on the stove let out a shrill whistle, its timely interruption giving Delilah a moment to pause her search.

"I'll be a strumming sunflower! I almost forgot the tea." She cracked a good-humored smirk.

As she headed to the kitchen, Daniel shifted closer to Olivia, their thighs nearly touching.

Olivia swallowed a bite of shortbread, and his gaze dropped helplessly to the flutter of her throat. He imagined grasping her hand again, running his thumb over her knuckles, his fingertips tracing the delicate skin.

Olivia watched him with a spirited glint in her eyes. "Care to share what's bouncing around in that brain of yours?"

Heat rushed his neck, but he held her gaze. "Guess I got a little distracted."

"By ..."

"Your hands, Ollie." He offered a self-deprecating chuckle. Her nickname tumbled out, like she was once again the close confidante of his youth. "I found myself utterly mesmerized by your hands."

"In the spirit of not getting distracted," she inched closer. "Perhaps you should hold them again."

Before he had a chance to react, she rubbed her palm against his.

He released a measured exhale, a jolt coursing through him as her fingers locked with his. Holding her soft hand, he stroked her knuckles with his thumb.

"Better focus now?" Olivia teased.

He obliged her teasing by a slight blush rising in his cheeks. "Mmhmm ..."

Delilah returned, precariously balancing a copper tray stacked with teacups, a teapot, and finger sandwiches. As she poured the tea and handed them the cups, the spicy floral scent of hibiscus perfumed the air.

A china cup slipped in her grasp, clattering against the tray.

"Oops!" she chuckled.

Daniel reluctantly released Olivia's hand, his skin instantly missing hers. He swallowed the scalding and distasteful tea, and thanked Delilah for agreeing to see them.

"Now, where were we? Ah yes, Lillian's gentleman caller from long ago." Plopping into a creaky wicker chair, Delilah's fingers twirled as if conjuring a download on her computer. "He was utterly taken with her. But then again, every guy was."

Olivia nibbled on a cucumber sandwich. "I wonder if he might be the man who recently sent Lillian a letter that arrived at my bookshop. There was no sender's identity listed on the envelope."

"Ooh, an anonymous sweetheart resurfacing after all these years?" Delilah clutched her heart. "How thrillingly romantic, sugar plum! True love is waiting patiently for the right moment."

"Think back to when you first learned about Lillian's unidentified suitor," Olivia said. "Did anyone hear him recount stories from his travels? Anything that might hint at his identity?"

Delilah's lips formed a thoughtful line while she twisted a gold bangle around her wrist. "Nothing that I can recall." She fidgeted, pulling on the bangle again, as if it brought her comfort. Her gaze drifted to the window, watching a bird flit by outside. After a moment, she refocused on Daniel and Olivia. "I'm afraid my memory fails me in the details."

As they dove back into questioning, Daniel watched Olivia tuck a silken strand of hair behind her ear, revealing the graceful slope of her neck.

His nerves simmered with awakened hunger.

He was falling deeper under her spell.

She was irresistible.

He took another sip of tea, then set the cup down with deliberate precision. "At first, we assumed he might be connected to a man we spotted yesterday. He was wearing a fedora. Slender build, sharp features."

"My nephew Elliot wears a fedora, though I haven't seen him in ages." Delilah operated in two modes: excessively cheerful, or curiously scatter-brained. One hand absently stroked the orange and green beaded necklace resting on her collarbone. "We were close when he was younger, even after his parents died and he had to go live with other relatives. He used to send me the most amusing postcards from his travels. I know he liked Austin, Texas. But then the postcards … stopped. I often wonder what became of him. He was always well-groomed and prided himself on his appearance."

"Your nephew's name is Elliot?"

"Yes."

"Last name?"

"Fitzwater. Elliot is my brother's son. Sadly, my brother passed away many years ago. He was wise and warm, and a true inspiration to our entire family. Elliot was devastated when he passed. We all were."

"Why does your nephew wear a fedora?"

A shimmer of reminiscence touched Delilah's pale green eyes. "When he was a young boy, he found his father's old fedora in the attic. It was worn and shabby at best, but he took a liking to it. Boasted that it made him look like a detective. It probably reminded him of his father. "

Her fingers traced an imaginary brim in the air. "From that day on, he wore it everywhere. Became a bit of a trademark for him. He said it brought him luck, memories of his father, and a touch of anonymity."

"Two guys with the same description. Two different names," Daniel whispered to Olivia.

"So odd," she agreed.

"Nora, the librarian, claimed he was a family friend, and the guy's name is Victor Steele," Daniel continued. "Is it possible that they know each other?"

"Nora and Elliot? How?" Delilah opened her mouth, then closed it again. "And who is Victor Steele?"

"That's what I'm asking."

The room fell into a contemplative silence, broken only by the faint creaking of the wicker chair as Delilah rocked back and forth.

Daniel propped his elbow on the armrest of the sofa. "Olivia, Nora, Theodore, and I might've seen your nephew by the fountain in town yesterday. He wore a fedora and handed Nora an envelope."

Delilah's eyebrows arched in a silent question. "What was in the envelope?"

"Nora was extremely evasive." Olivia's fingers grazed over the woven fabric of the embroidered pillow. "Before any of us reacted, he disappeared into one of the buildings, and Nora left shortly afterward."

Delilah turned; her gaze anchored on a photo. "Last I heard, my nephew was somewhere chasing his dreams. Can't tie him down, that one."

"Is this him?" Daniel stood and retrieved the photo from an end table. He held it up, revealing a handsome young man with sharp features.

Delilah affirmed with a subtle inclination of her head. "Who else? I never married or had children of my own."

"This man isn't wearing a fedora, but the photo looks like the guy we saw with Nora," Olivia said. "The resemblance—"

"Is uncanny," Daniel finished.

Were they about to unravel decades of answers? Or did an eerie coincidence cast more fog along the trail?

"Would your nephew have contacted you if he had arrived in town?" Olivia asked.

Delilah's response came with a nonchalant shrug. "Not necessarily."

Anticipation rippled through Daniel like an electric hum, though he tempered it with an easy grin. Had Elliot changed his name to Victor? Unlikely, but anything was possible.

He returned the photo to the table. The cushions sank beneath him as he sat back next to Olivia. A clock chimed from the next room while the sun's last rays washed over a shelf of disarrayed trinkets.

"Your nephew didn't know Lillian?" Daniel pressed. His fingers drummed a silent rhythm on the armrest.

"They're decades apart in age." Delilah's gaze wandered over to a bookshelf, as if seeking answers. "Unless we're talking about two separate men. My nephew's name is Elliot."

Olivia, teacup in hand, gestured toward Delilah. "He wouldn't have changed his name?"

"Of course not."

The room stilled, the reality of the situation sinking in. Deflated, Daniel put his head in his hands, because another one of their leads had been smashed. No evidence tied youthful Elliot to sophisticated elder Lillian.

Therefore, Elliot couldn't be the enigmatic man from Lillian's past. He was young enough to be her son.

But did he have a twin?

If so, it meant reevaluating the entire situation from square one.

After they left Delilah's home with more dead ends, Olivia's expression carried a hint of irony. "Why did we assume her nephew had to be our guy when we saw the photo?" she asked.

"We got ahead of ourselves because he looked so similar

to Victor. We should verify facts before chasing assumptions."

Daniel's mind whirled with the various individuals potentially tied to the Lillian mystery. There was Elliot Fitzwater, Delilah's nephew, who bore a striking resemblance to the mysterious man named Victor Steele who knew Nora, the town's librarian. Nora herself had been evasive about her relationship with Victor.

And then there was the complication of Theodore and Emma.

Somehow, Daniel felt that unraveling the connections between all these people was crucial to uncovering Lillian's romantic past.

"Elliot Fitzwater appears to have no direct ties to Lillian, despite his resemblance to Victor Steele," Olivia reiterated.

"True. But does Victor somehow factor into the decades-old letter?"

"The question of the day," Olivia replied.

They passed Sweetwater Springs elementary school, and Olivia centered her attention on an advertisement seeking volunteers for the reading program.

"I always wished for more programs like this when I was young," she remarked.

"I've seen you volunteering here through the classroom window."

"How?" She turned to him. "Have you been spying on me?"

"I've lived in town for a while and pass by this way often. A class of fourth graders was smiling at your dramatic story-telling style. From what I gathered; your encouraging spirit has made quite an impact."

She grinned. "Since you already caught me in the act, I'll keep up with my schoolroom readings whenever I can."

Daniel noted the slight reddening in her cheeks as she

adjusted the advertisement. He appreciated her efforts to make their community a better place.

When they were in their teens, she collaborated with nursery schools to be a guest storyteller. Dressed as characters from the stories, she made reading interactive and fun, and he knew she left a lasting impression on the young minds.

He pictured her now, her chestnut hair pulled back but tendrils escaping as she animated her face and voice, pulling the children into magical worlds.

"I have no doubt you'll keep brightening those kids' days. Are you still organizing book donation drives?"

She nodded. "A couple of times a year."

In high school, she'd collected gently used books from the community and distributed them to families, ensuring more children had the opportunity to explore the magic of reading.

"More and more things to love about you." He put an arm around her waist and captured her lips in a tender kiss.

He said the word. Love. She didn't answer, save for a sharp inhale.

He tucked her arm through his, and they continued walking.

As more memories of her altruistic effort lingered in Daniel's mind, a black sedan rolled by them, slowing as it passed, shiny hubcaps flashing in the sunlight.

Daniel stopped, tented his eyes, and stared.

Could it be …? He blinked hard, his heart pounding.

The driver's sharp profile and brimmed fedora hat resembled Elliot's, Victor's, or whoever it was.

The passenger seat's window cracked open. With a silent gasp, Nora's gaze met Daniel's before she slumped down, out of sight.

He stood as immobile as a statue while the car accelerated and sped down the street.

Olivia gripped his hand and passed him a cautious glance. "Was that Nora?" At his stunned nod, her eyes flared. "Does Elliot have a brother named Victor? If so, wouldn't Delilah have mentioned him?"

Adrenaline flooded Daniel's veins.

Perhaps.

Or perhaps his exhausted eyes were deceiving him.

CHAPTER 8

*S*everal days later, the last rays of sunlight scattered through the historical society's windows as Olivia blew dust off a decades-old high school yearbook.

She cracked it open. The musty scent of aged paper and binding glue filled her nostrils.

She and Daniel had been searching the archives for hours in search of clues tying the elusive threads connecting Lillian, Elliot, Victor, and the romantic letter writer.

As she combed through the yearbook, pointing out evidence linking young Theodore and Lillian, Daniel's phone buzzed. She surreptitiously observed the number, noting it was an overseas call. Earlier, his phone had buzzed twice, though he had ignored it.

Brows stitched together, Daniel excused himself and answered his cellphone in hushed tones, growing increasingly urgent. Despite Olivia's attempt to give him privacy, his rigid, squared posture alarmed her. She overheard fragmented phrases as he paced.

"Incident … shipment … authorities interrogating …"

Her blood turned to ice at his anguished exclamation,

"Stolen?! That ancient limestone tablet was bound for the British Museum exhibit opening."

Her inquisitive gaze met his shell-shocked expression once he ended the call.

Before she asked any questions, he brushed past her, muttering about phoning a coworker—leaving her reeling with speculation over what globe spanning project had apparently gone awry.

What did it signal about his priorities between adventures abroad and settling in their small hometown?

She stood and pushed aside the yearbook, her appetite for further romantic clues spoiled by fresh doubts.

What exactly was Daniel involved with? Why were authorities grilling him?

Deep furrows creased his forehead at the mention of some precious artifact being stolen. Was he not as far removed from his international work as she had assumed?

When he returned, Olivia fisted her hands on her hips. "Are you in some type of legal trouble abroad?" she asked.

He pressed his palms against the table, his grip so tight that his knuckles whitened. "There are suspicions my team broke laws in obtaining an artifact, but I swear we thoroughly vetted the dealer."

"Is it serious?"

"It could be, considering that they can't find the tablet." He lifted his hands. "However, my time away made me realize none of it matters more than you, Ollie. I previously informed them I'm through and gave my notice. I'll sort this mess out when I return home for good."

She thought he had already done that. Returned home for good.

Though he seemed genuinely contrite, unease ensnared her. Could she trust that he had truly left his other world behind? She hadn't realized anything about his profession was questionable until now. Or might the lure of adventure and acclaim eventually tear him away again, no matter the promises?

She struggled to keep her composure while his explanations flew by. He was withdrawing from global work, he insisted. Nothing mattered except for her.

Since he'd left, she'd become adept at keeping anything she truly liked under wraps. And she really liked him. Loved him, in fact.

Tears blurred her vision. Juggling her bookshop responsibilities and delving into the mystery of Lillian's letter writer was demanding enough. She didn't want to deal with Daniel's catastrophes.

Clearing her tight throat, she flipped to the yearbook page where she had left off and avoided his unspoken attempts to read her shuttered mood.

"Look here," she finally said, settling on a chair by the bookshelves. "I found this high school yearbook from the 1950s with photos of a young Lillian." She pointed out the images, paging rapidly to reveal more details.

"She's so pretty." Daniel stood behind her and peered over her shoulder at the black-and-white photos captioned in fine cursive. There was Lillian, glowing, curls pinned to the side, and a mischievous smile hinting at adventures yet to come.

Olivia turned the page.

As if scorched, her fingers recoiled from the image of a gangly, earnest-looking teenage boy posing in thick spectacles beneath a tousle of hair.

"Theodore Weatherly, the Third," Daniel read aloud. "He's in the yearbook, too. I figured he and Lillian must've attended high school together."

"The dates add up. I neglected to mention that during my visit to the library's newspaper archives, I stumbled on an article about a Theodore Weatherly. He donated funds for a new library wing and was friends with Lillian's father, Arthur Beaumont. Judging from the dates, he was Theodore's grandfather."

"Interesting connection." Daniel pointed to the young Theodore's image. "Any idea why he might be called the third?"

"It could be a family tradition, like passing down names through generations. Or maybe it's a nickname or a title. What do you think?"

"Hard to say. It's possible that there is significance behind 'the third' we're not aware of." Daniel leaned over and whispered in her ear. "Could Theodore be our man?"

"From the students' comments, he seemed like a shy, quiet guy. He and Lillian were bound like bookends—tutoring each other after school, jitterbugging at the dance hall, and sharing root beer floats at the soda fountain in town."

Could her old friend harbor this long-held secret of being in love with Lillian? She envisioned a gangly Theodore scribbling poetic lines to his sweetheart on folded paper.

Olivia flagged the entry in the yearbook, her conviction growing.

After additional hours of mining ledgers and microfiche articles well into the evening, Olivia switched off the lights. As they secured the building, Daniel's gaze found hers. They both recognized it—perhaps the answer was at last within reach.

SEVERAL DAYS LATER, on a Sunday afternoon, Olivia and Daniel strolled on the outskirts of Sweetwater Springs. A belated gust of wind carried the crisp, earthy scent of April.

Though her quest to unearth Lillian's romantic history

continued to occupy Olivia's mind, she stole more frequent moments with Daniel.

Moments to wander sleepy neighborhoods thick with evergreens, conversing about everything and nothing the way they did as childhood friends. The chaos of life slowed whenever they were together, as if the universe sighed, "There you are ... isn't this better?"

She leaned into his sturdy frame and tucked a strand of her wildly fluttering hair behind her ear. Despite her efforts, she could never quite wrangle those unruly curls into submission.

"You should wear green more often." Daniel eyed the silk blouse she wore under her cropped cotton cardigan, the floral pattern reminiscent of a garden in full bloom. "The color brings out the warmth in your eyes."

Olivia grinned, a spark of exhilaration igniting at his closeness. His compliments and unfaltering presence through the trials of this quest made her feel like she could conquer the entire world if he stood nearby.

"Should I now?" Amusement laced her words.

"Purely an impartial observation. Emerald green suits you."

"Mmhmm ... emerald green." Olivia bit back a smile, enjoying this flustered side of him. "Are you admitting that you don't like my usual choices and colors?"

"What? No, I didn't ..." He faltered as she laughed.

"I'm only teasing." She bumped his shoulder good-humoredly. "Thank you for the compliment. I may start taking your fashion advice more often."

His expression relaxed into an easy grin. "In that case, I stand by my words. You look beautiful in green, Ollie."

She expressed her gratitude by grasping his hand, drawing out the touch as she traced her fingertips over his palm.

He flushed.

"Distracted again?" Her fingers wandered to the inside of his wrist.

His breath hitched. "You have that effect on me."

Chuckling, she curled against him, snuggling into the warmth of his shoulder as he pressed a kiss into her hair. He wrapped an arm securely around her waist, grazing the sliver of bare skin where her shirt had ridden up slightly.

Her mind wandered to their latest intriguing discoveries, and their intriguing past, their hearts connected like the fine strands of a spider web, fragile yet resilient in the face of adversity.

"Theodore and Lillian were an item several decades ago," she said. "What do you make of those odds?"

"Lillian had her fair share of beaus, and Theodore was obviously one of them, so the odds are excellent. Have you confronted him yet?"

"I honestly don't know how to bring up the subject."

"Have you noticed the way Theodore's face lights up whenever someone mentions Lillian's name?"

"I haven't."

"Well, I have. It seems more than friendly fondness for an old girlfriend."

"Nora, Victor, and Elliot are still in the mix, and I've gone round and round about it." Olivia plucked a trailing vine spilling with vibrant wildflowers, twirling the blooms in her hand. "My instinct says our next move should be discovering why those men look so strikingly alike. It feels like the key to explaining Nora's secrecy, too."

Daniel paused and rested his hands on her shoulders. The low sunset cast his rugged features in a burnished glow, and her breath murmured in admiration.

"How about this? I'll fold up a picnic dinner for us and meet you at the archives room at the historical society building tomorrow night," he said. "We'll continue to research."

She grinned. "Is it okay to use the facilities after hours?"

"I'm the new president of the society, and I say it's fine. These days, I'm there most of the time."

"Sure, then." Her grin broke into a laugh. "I'll bring deviled eggs. I found my grandmother's recipe."

"Deal, and I can't wait to try them. Tomorrow night, after you close the bookshop, meet me there. However long it takes, we'll try to piece together the truth."

A deep affection fluttered—an enduring gratitude for the genuine connection she had discovered with this handsome and extraordinary man.

Her fluttering spirits sank as she spotted his pretty ex, Vanessa, from high school. She exited a boutique and crossed the street.

Vanessa's adventurous spirit had always shared Daniel's wanderlust more than Olivia's self-contained life. Would the reminder spark old feelings for him? Were these brief reunited days a closure before he resumed the path meant for him beyond sleepy Sweetwater Springs?

Sometimes past dreams whispered loudest when one's future hung balanced between faith and fear, and the sudden threat of old flames rekindled.

When her knees forgot to bend and she feared she couldn't walk another step, Daniel's strong hand tipped her face upward.

"You own my heart, Ollie. No fancy promises that fade away like dust in some distant place."

He realized what she was thinking. His earnest words resonated through her tangled fears.

His hazel eyes blazed with conviction. "I'm referring to roots. Deep roots. Your voice, from when we were kids, guided me back. Will you trust me, no matter what happens?"

"I trust you. Only don't make me chase you halfway across the world before you realize you belong here with me."

"You'll chase me? You, the homebody?"

Under the onset of shimmering stars, Olivia replied with boldness. She drew him into a fierce kiss, intent on her answer.

Yes.

CHAPTER 9

$\mathcal{L}$ ater the next evening, Olivia, toting a woven basket, entered the historical society building. Inside the basket, she'd placed a cooler containing deviled eggs and a fruit and cheese board. She wore a floor-length, flower-patterned maxi skirt, and the skirt flowed with every step. For practicality, she chose comfortable ankle boots with a low heel, ensuring stability on uneven ground. Tying the look together, she paired the skirt with a long-sleeved sweater, mismatched socks, and a linen shawl packed in her tote bag.

She found Daniel sorting through a stack of papers at a solid oak table, looking devastatingly handsome in the muted lighting. His navy-blue collared shirt, tucked into fitted jeans, flattered his tall, athletic frame. His forearms were exposed as he rolled up the sleeves, revealing toned muscles that hinted at his active, outdoorsy lifestyle. She imagined those capable arms pulling her close as they shared a slow dance under the moonlight, his work-hewn fingers tilting her chin upward, finding her lips for a kiss.

His dark hair was attractively windswept, as if he had run

his hands through it while buried in research. He had draped a brown leather jacket over the back of his chair, and she caught a glimpse of sturdy hiking boots sticking out from where he was sitting.

She drew in a fortifying breath, temporarily speechless at the sight of him. She forced herself to pry her eyes away and set her tote bag and woven basket on the floor.

"Hi, gorgeous." He smiled, stood, and kissed her. "Did you drive here?"

"I walked. I have my car, but I hardly ever use it these days because everything in town is so close."

"I have news. I may be onto something explaining Theodore's background."

"What is it?" she asked, as they both pulled up a chair, sitting side by side.

He rifled through a stack of yellowed documents. "Here." He slid a photograph to her—a portrait of a refined gentleman, head held high and shoulders back, displaying a book bearing the family name 'Weatherly.'

"Theodore Weatherly, the First," Olivia read aloud. "He wrote poetry?"

"Highly esteemed poetry, from the looks of it. His son carried on the literary tradition impressively." Daniel arranged another framed photo, this of a young man clad in expertly crafted trousers and a tailored blazer, holding a tome of verse penned under Weatherly.

"Theodore Weatherly, the Second," Daniel said. "Both father and son made a mark on the poetry scene, which explains the inherited nickname for our dear friend Theodore."

In amazement, Olivia stared at the photos. "Theodore comes from a long line of esteemed poets. I wonder if he ever got published."

"Let's find out." Daniel disappeared into the aisles, soon to reemerge with a sizable scrapbook. He brushed off the traces of spider silk and handed it to her.

They leafed through newspaper clippings of Theodore's grandfather's and father's accomplishments. Interspersed were essays citing accolades from poetry competitions.

"Well, I'll be." Daniel tapped his finger on a particular passage. "Says here, a former US Poet Laureate and literary society patron developed a keen interest in the elder Theodore's work. Even awarded him a significant cash prize that made headlines."

The emergence of a prosperous poetic lineage transformed Theodore's identity as "the third" from an odd curiosity into a rightful inheritance.

Olivia sat back. "Our unassuming friend. Who dreamed he carried such a rich legacy?"

If only seventeen-year-old Lillian could have anticipated what her introverted boyfriend had blossomed into thanks to his literary accomplishments.

As Daniel reviewed more documents, Olivia fixated on his rugged profile—the set line of his jaw, the unrestrained admiration lighting his handsome face when he turned and met her gaze.

"You know," she pondered aloud, "you should wear more blue. It turns your hazel eyes into a mirror of the summer sky."

"Is that so?" Amusement sparked a twinkle at the corners of those eyes. "And here I thought you preferred me in green."

"Your compliment for me, remember?" Her lips curved into a huge smile. "But as long as I get to admire the view, what does it matter?"

"The view, hmm?" He inched nearer. "Far be it from me to deny a lady's wishes."

His voice caressed her, rich and smooth, sending delicious shivers down her spine. She angled toward him as the air between them changed, grew charged, alive with possibility.

A noise from the hall made her pause. A window rattling, perhaps, or a creaking door.

"Most likely a draft coming from somewhere." He drew away, the romantic moment broken, though his eyes glimmered with something intimate and heated.

He stood and restored the documents to their respective locations on the shelves. His gaze met hers, a silent message to stay still.

He crept toward the door, dragged it open, and peered down the hallway. She strained to listen, but the only sound was Daniel's footsteps.

"Nothing there," he said after a moment.

His grip on the latch was tight.

"Are you certain?" she asked.

"This is an old building, and there are normal sounds as the place settles at night. I've been here many times. No cause for alarm." His assurance brought a lightness to her chest as he flipped off the lights. "Is it time for our picnic?"

She grabbed her tote bag and basket. "Absolutely. I'm starved."

"And I'm always hungry." He tugged on his jacket and smiled. "I drove my car here. Let's head to the park."

As they stepped outside, she peered up. The sky had transitioned into a canvas of nuanced hues, oranges and pinks, and deeper shades of blue.

She grabbed her shawl from her tote bag, and he wrapped it around her shoulders.

They arrived shortly afterwards, and Daniel parked at the curb.

The park took on a distinct character at night, with the radiance of street lamps and pale yellow stars.

He brought along a battery-powered lantern to light the picnic area, as well as a cooler and thick, fleecy blanket. They unfolded the blanket, choosing a sheltered corner over-looking a small pond. The pond glimmered beneath a faint moon; its surface occasionally stippled by the circular ripples of a fish's quiet splash.

The isolated quacking of ducks and the rhythmic chirping of birds created a tranquil background. Dew clung to the lush layer of grass, its blades glistening with droplets of moisture.

"Our discovery tonight calls for a toast," Daniel proclaimed, pouring sparkling grape cider into paper cups as they situated themselves on the blanket.

"Wait until you taste my deviled eggs. I added a special ingredient."

"What?"

"Paprika!"

"Don't they sell paprika in all the grocery stores?"

"This is smoked paprika. The flavor is more intense." Olivia arranged the eggs on small plates, garnished with dill. As she showcased a spread that included a cheese and cracker board and a fruit platter boasting slices of water-melon and juicy berries, she raised her cup. "To standing on the shoulders of history."

"And smoked paprika. He took a bite of the deviled egg. "This is delicious!" He tapped his cup lightly against hers. "And a toast to Theodore the Third and my beautiful Ollie."

No sly flirtation or overplayed charm. He had a simple and genuine interest in her; and he didn't hide it.

"Are you still superstitious?" He studied her socks. "Do the socks bring you good luck?"

"Some superstitions die hard. Now I wear them out of

habit. Or, if I'm honest with myself, it's a fun way to break away from routine."

He set down his cup and moved closer. "Shall we continue?"

"With what?"

"With what we started in the historical society building."

"What was that?"

"A kiss."

She set down her cup, too. Dragging a ragged breath, she raised her face to within an inch of his. His tongue grazed her lips, coaxing them to open, and she welcomed the invitation.

"I'm glad you're here with me. This is where you belong." His lips came down on hers with a challenging resolve. The kiss deepened, sending honeyed tendrils of longing down her spine.

Minutes later, he lifted his mouth. Tenderly, his thumbs stroked her flaming cheeks. She stirred, and he held her closer.

"Don't move yet, Ollie. I want to stretch this moment out longer."

She placed a hand on his arm and gazed up at him—his strong, dark eyebrows, his features sculpted with a blend of strength and refinement. He had such an effect on her. He drew her in irresistibly.

"What's going on behind that handsome face of yours?" she asked.

"I was remembering when we came here as kids." He turned his palm to enfold her hand in his. "Part of me always saw us ending up like this, together on a starlit night, and there's nowhere else I'd rather be in the entire world. That held true then, and it holds true now."

The sheer yearning in his voice caused her pulse to race

madly. His words resonated, a confirmation of her reawakening—a thousand moonbeams, bright and shiny.

"Daniel. I've wanted this moment, too." She sat up straighter and spoke louder. She wished for him to hear every word. "Maybe dreams come true. I'm thankful to have you back in my life."

He smiled, a world of implicit promises shining in his eyes. For several perfect moments under a starlit sky, they lingered in a shared understanding.

Their love for each other had never faded.

Eventually, she turned the conversation to their latest breakthrough, eager to hear his take.

"I bet Emma is aware of Theodore's family history," she began, her words breaking the spell of their connection. "She's totally plugged into him. I'll ask her."

"Good idea." Daniel downed his second cup of cider in one swig. "Theodore evidently doesn't want anyone to recognize his accomplishments."

"Most people shout an honorary title from the rooftops. He became much better off financially than the townsfolk realized after those poetry prizes and royalties. Yet he lives humbly."

"It's possible that he values humility. His desire for a meaningful life goes beyond material wealth." Daniel reached for a slice of watermelon. "Now what about Elliot, Victor, and Nora?"

"They may have nothing to do with Lillian," Olivia replied.

"Those three people have certainly complicated matters. Especially the strange resemblance between the two men. Delilah insisted the guy in the photo was her nephew, Elliot, yet we met Victor face-to-face. It makes you wonder if they're the same person."

An hour later, she poured herself another cup of cider. As

she and Daniel shared more bites from the fruit and cheese platter, she picked up a wedge of creamy Brie, savoring its smooth texture, and couldn't resist expressing a subtle "mmm" of approval.

In the middle of their discussion, Daniel's voice trailed off as he stared past her. She followed his gaze to see none other than the pair of men they'd been discussing.

She assumed the men were Elliot and Victor, side-by-side in an amiable conversation, although one of them had a noticeable limp and held a lit cigarette.

In the light, their resemblances were unmistakable.

Both dressed stylishly. One wore slim grey slacks with a charcoal blazer over a burgundy button-down, adding a polished accent to his features. The other sported midnight-blue jeans and a black leather jacket over a dark turtleneck, the monochromatic palette offsetting deep brown eyes.

Olivia gripped Daniel's arm. "Talk about coincidence."

He lifted his chin in acknowledgement as they both came to their feet.

"They could be reflections of each other," he said. "What are they doing here?"

One man raised a hand in greeting, his movements exuding effortless confidence.

"Hello." He flashed a disarming smile, the corners of his eyes crinkling in a manner that hinted at a mischievous streak under the refined exterior. He exuded a feline smoothness, from the way his polished dress shoes glided through the grass to the casual drape of his blazer over a single shoulder.

"I'm Elliot Fitzwater." He extended a hand before gesturing to the other man. "And this is Victor."

Olivia stiffened, struggling to make sense of it all.

"Victor Steele." The tip of the cherry-red ember of Victor's cigarette flared. He took a final drag, then, with a deliberate yet relaxed motion, disposed of it, grinding it out under his heel. A hiss accompanied the extinguished flame, and the faint aroma of tobacco lingered in his wake. There was a worldly weariness to his indifference. "You met me the other day."

She gaped.

Before the silence stretched too long, Daniel extended a polite nod. "You've both been the topic of conversation lately."

"Why?" Victor asked.

"You're kidding … For starters, you resemble—"

"Twins separated at birth?" Victor suggested, earning an awkward pause.

"Uh, yes, as a matter of fact."

"We aren't brothers."

Finally, Olivia found her voice. "Then who are you both, exactly?"

"How about we explain?"

Olivia gave Daniel an imperceptible nod. If they stayed standing, she reasoned, a quick exit was possible if these guys made any odd movements.

Daniel's brow furrowed as he studied them. "Very well."

How did two people resemble each other so closely, from the dark eyes, closer to black than brown, to the sharp jaws?

Upon further examination, though, Victor limped. Elliot didn't.

Victor smoked. Elliot didn't.

She filed the details away, landmarks amidst the dizzying identicalness, and turned to Elliot. "We visited Delilah Fitzwater, and she swore that the man in the photograph at her home was you."

"My aunt is right."

"But we also met Victor by the fountain."

"There is history bonding us together." Elliot gestured to

Victor. "A while ago, Victor and I each did one of those trendy genetic tests mapping out ancestral lineages. We didn't know each other at that point. However, we discovered we had links to this town with likely origins and extended relatives floating out there somewhere."

As Elliot spoke, Olivia mused aloud. "Are you long lost cousins?"

"Once our matches aligned, the website encouraged us to email each other. We did, and I wrote it off as mere coincidence that my map overlapped with Victor." Elliot rocked back on his heels; hands tucked in his pockets. There was an affable, down-to-earth quality about him, despite his refined outward appearance. "I wasted no time tracking down my newly discovered relative."

Victor leaned against the tree trunk, his posture radiating a quiet intensity. His gaze was penetrating and assessing.

"I spent nearly six months emailing familial matches from the site, plugging my details into genealogy forums," he said. Meticulous and driven, he seemed the type of man who didn't rest until he uncovered every scrap of elusive truth.

"How are you two related?" Daniel inquired.

Elliot gazed across the dark pond, a sliver of moonlight illuminating a slight ripple of waves. "We share a great-great-grandfather—a farmer who married a girl from the next town over in 1878."

Daniel let out a slow whistle, his breath fogging the chilly night air.

"Our planned meeting brought us face-to-face." Victor shifted his attention to Elliot. "You were looking for more bloody Fitzwater's while I was trying to find any Sweetwater-tied Steeles."

"What about Nora?" Olivia asked Victor. "You were driving, and she seemed to hide. Why the secrecy?"

He grinned. "How did you figure out it was me and not Elliot?"

"Nora's reaction made me assume the driver was you since we'd witnessed your interaction by the fountain," Olivia replied. "How did you come to meet her?"

"Elliot remembered her from when he lived in Sweetwater Springs. When we bumped into her, she immediately put two and two together," Victor explained. "First, she assisted with the genealogy hunt, and then she interrogated Elliot about his relatives. She wanted to keep it confidential until she figured out how to connect us. The envelope I passed to her contained additional information from the ancestry website."

"She's lovely, isn't she?" Elliot chuckled softly, a roguish sparkle in his eye. His far-off gaze suggested a man easily infatuated and distracted by a pretty face. "I wouldn't mind to getting to know her better. When we were young, we played hide and seek in a maple grove by a stream, and I teased her about making maple syrup. We gathered fallen leaves once, and I gave her a bouquet. I wonder if she remembers."

Olivia's mind whirled as she attempted to piece together the puzzle.

"Have either of you heard of a woman named Lillian Beaumont?"

"Nope." Victor answered quickly.

Elliot paused. "I remember the Beaumont family. They were wealthy, right?"

A flicker of trepidation stirred in her gut—if their ancestral ties truly reached back to Sweetwater Springs' historic roots, might they know more than they were letting on?

Olivia turned again to Elliot. "Is Delilah, your aunt, aware of Victor?"

"Not yet, although I plan to introduce him soon."

She reflected on the unpredictable twists securing these lives together across time and chance. "She'll be overjoyed by this sudden expansion of her family."

"IT'S ALL PECULIAR, THOUGH," Daniel said later, after Victor and Elliot had left. "On the surface, their reunion seems plausible enough. But years of archeological work have taught me to question even the most innocent of accepted narratives. I can't quell the nagging unease that more layers remain hidden beneath these supposed cousins."

"Why is it peculiar to have distant relatives? With all these ancestry tests nowadays, it's probably more common than we think," Olivia replied. "I imagine Victor and Elliot inherited the signature family traits—dark brown eyes, thick eyebrows, and sharp profiles. Dominant genes, I suppose. Up close and side by side, they don't look or act nearly as alike."

She perched closer to Daniel, a novel consideration stirring.

The men had glossed over their backstories. Could more information still mushroom beneath their charming, parallel grins?

Olivia packed the leftover fruit, cheese, and crackers while Daniel folded the picnic blanket. As she handed him the last of the containers and he strode to his car, voices drifted from a path nearby.

She recoiled for a beat. Then she strained to listen to the low-toned dialogue.

"... do you think they believed us?" Victor's tone floated through the darkness.

"Hard to say ..." came Elliot's measured response.

Olivia edged closer, curiosity spiking.

"Daniel is suspicious," Victor said. "And Olivia—she sees too much."

A twig snapped under her foot, and the indistinct murmurs instantly cut off.

Her heart hammered as she remained perfectly still. She tried to hear more, but their voices dropped to garbled whispers, and their footsteps disappeared.

A chill skated down Olivia's spine as Victor's words echoed in her mind:

"Daniel is suspicious of us, and Olivia sees too much."

Her pulse picked up tempo as her earlier wariness now proved justified. What did they have to hide? And why the act of deception over what should be an innocent family disclosure?

She sped back to help Daniel finish gathering their things, relaying the men's conversation to him.

A muscle ticked in his jaw as he absorbed Olivia's frantic whispers.

"So, my instincts have been correct all along," he said. "Something isn't adding up."

"I think you're right."

"Their motivations go beyond bonding over a newly discovered ancestral link. You know better than to take everything at face value, Ollie. Don't believe everything until you have examined every detail."

His words echoed the precision of an archaeologist's methodical approach.

Olivia sighed, realizing this was the opening round of what might develop into an intricate web of intrigue.

CHAPTER 10

The following morning, a rich sunrise highlighted the storefront windows. The sky, a canvas of muted grays and occasional hints of serene blue, set the stage for another day of ever-changing weather—a tango between brief sunlight and passing showers.

Olivia hurried her steps, intent on confirming suspicions regarding Theodore's love for Lillian. When her name was mentioned, the smile that creased his lips and his tender tone when he spoke about her, hinted at a deeper connection.

Butterflies swirled in Olivia's stomach as she pushed the wooden door of *Blissful Bites* open, and the bell above her head chimed. Inside, Emma's bakery unfolded like a confectionery wonderland. Stacked on rolling racks, flaky croissants shared space with dainty éclairs that glistened with glaze.

Emma, behind the counter, greeted Olivia.

Olivia stepped forward, noting the empty tables. "It's quiet today."

"I guarantee things will be crazy in a couple of hours."

Emma tucked her blond hair more securely under a white hair net. "My chocolate donuts aren't ready yet. Sorry."

"No worries." Olivia struggled to keep her tone casual. "By the way, have you noticed anything … between Theodore and Lillian?"

Emma, her expression serene, continued arranging a tray of delicate fruit tarts topped with vibrant berries. "Like what?"

"I can't help but believe that there's something more to their relationship."

"They're both regular customers who enjoy their pastries, but nothing out of the ordinary."

"Do they ever actually see each other?" Olivia asked.

"Not that I'm aware. They're on different schedules," Emma replied. "Besides, Lillian only moved back here recently."

"The way Theodore mentions her name, the look in his eyes, it's almost as if …"

"As if he's in love with her," Emma finished softly.

"Exactly. And I think he might be the unidentified sender of Lillian's letter."

When Emma didn't respond, Olivia continued. "Theodore is like a father figure to you, correct?"

"He is extremely kind."

"You would know if anyone would. Did he ever have a … a thing for Lillian?"

"Every guy had a thing for Lillian back in the day."

"Theodore in particular?"

"Take a number. Like I said, everyone." Emma finished arranging the tarts, then traced the edge of her flour-dusted apron. "Have you ever heard of a certain man named Clement Aubergine?"

Olivia squinted. Could he have been the man who had

penned the unidentified letter? She didn't recall any students by that name in the yearbook. Perhaps he was an upper-classman.

"Lillian and I have never discussed her past," Olivia replied. "Did Clement live in Sweetwater Springs?"

"Indeed." Emma's hands stilled. "He dated Lillian on and off. I heard tales of when they first met. She was the talk of the town, and I remember my mother saying that Clement was smitten from the moment he laid eyes on Lillian."

"What happened between them?"

"Life, I suppose." Emma offered a ghost of a smile. "Lillian had dreams of traveling the world, and Clement wanted to settle down. In the end, they went their separate ways, but some wonder if either ever truly moved on."

"Does Clement still live in Sweetwater Springs?"

"Last I heard, he lives at the senior facility. But then he may have moved away years ago. I'm not entirely sure."

"He lives at the facility in town," Olivia clarified.

"Supposedly, that's one possibility."

"Has Lillian gone to see him?"

"No idea." As Emma elaborated on the man's romantic entanglements with Lillian, Olivia's imagination spun loose. Perhaps an exciting new contender who had written the letter waited in the wings. She'd need to modify her suspicions.

She glanced at the clock on the wall, realizing she had lost track of time. The morning rush would soon begin, and she didn't want to keep Emma from her work.

"Thank you for your help," she said. "I appreciate you taking a few minutes to chat with me."

Emma's smile was gentle, causing her eyes to crease at the edges in a heartwarming expression. "Anytime. You can always find me here."

With a grateful nod, Olivia exited the bakery and stepped

onto the sidewalk. As she inhaled, the morning air filled her lungs with freshness. The sun had climbed higher in the sky, casting a bright light on the quaint facades of the storefronts and houses that lined the street.

She glided back to her shop, her mind swirling with considerations of Theodore, Lillian, Clement, and the mysterious letter. As she stepped inside, the familiar scent of old books and the faint trace of vanilla from the scented candle on a bookshelf greeted her. The floorboards groaned as she walked to the front counter, each step a comforting reminder of the shop's history.

In a burst of contemplation, she watched the recognizable town unfold before her—passersby with scampering strides, the occasional clatter of a bicycle wheel on cobblestone streets, and picturesque scenes she knew by heart.

THE FOLLOWING DAY, Olivia could hardly focus on cataloguing a stack of books. Between this latest person, Clement Aubergine, and all the others who might've written the letter to Lillian, her mind reran the puzzling conversation she'd overheard between Victor and Elliot.

After further discussion with Daniel, they concluded the two men were seeking a large sum of cash tied to an inheritance somewhere in Sweetwater Springs' history.

As Daniel quietly noted, many paths in life led back to only one thing. Money.

As she tidied the shop, movement flickered at the edge of her vision, and she tamped down her startled reaction. Fear was a destination she had grown reluctant to revisit.

Fortunately, it was merely a stray newspaper tumbling down the street.

She resumed re-shelving novels at double speed and checked her watch. Time to close.

She found herself drawn to the bookshelves, her fingers itching to uncover any hidden clues. She ran her hand along the spines of the old books, the rough texture of the worn paper and the faint musty smell filling her senses. Each book held a story, a piece of history, or the imaginings of the future.

The shop bell jangled violently. She whirled around as the door flung wide, a strong wind gusting across the threshold. Curious. She could've sworn the door was secure.

She crossed the shop to seal the door, double checking the lock. As the deadbolt clicked, the lamps flickered.

Were those footsteps creaking upstairs where she kept the extra inventory?

Surely not.

"Hello …?" She rubbed her arms brusquely, willing away imaginary stares, peering down aisles for anything amiss. She stepped to the front window and looked out when tires crunched outside.

There stood Victor, or Elliot, emerging sleek as a panther from a black luxury car. His charcoal-gray suit, expertly tailored, accentuated his lean frame. Their eyes locked through the glass as he limped toward the door.

Victor.

She unlocked the door, vowing not to let her guard down for a minute. "Hello … Victor, right?"

"Yes."

"Can I help find you something? I'm closing shop for the day."

Why had he sought her out? And with such an entrance, he was clearly a man accustomed to showy theatrics and keeping folks off balance.

"I'm not here for any books, and I won't keep you long."

He wasn't wearing a fedora. He hadn't worn a fedora the other night, either. In fact, neither had Elliot.

"May I ask you something?" She returned to stand behind the counter.

He limped to the counter and leaned against it. "By all means."

"What is it with this fedora? First, you wore it everywhere. And now neither you nor Elliot wear one. What gives?"

"Elliot wore a fedora ever since he was a boy, when he found his late father's hat in the attic. He adopted it as a lucky charm."

She monitored him, cloaking her wariness with a façade of casual interest. "His Aunt Delilah elaborated on those details when Daniel and I visited her."

"So, you know I'm not lying." Victor's eyes locked onto hers. "When I first arrived, I took a style cue from him and picked up my fedora to match his signature look."

"If surreptitious was the goal, consider it achieved."

"We looked like twins from an old detective movie, though we attracted more puzzled gapes than I expected. For me, blending into the community is more prudent."

"You are making such a charming attempt to prove you are related," Olivia said, inclining her head.

He smirked. "Just long-lost relatives, reunited by chance."

She fought back a smile at his audaciousness. "What brings you here, Victor Steele?"

He paused, a man with piercing dark eyes, and she realized those eyes only revealed a fraction of his thoughts. His gaze swept over the bookshop, as if absorbing every detail.

"I wanted to speak to you about the other night in the park." His voice carried a measured cadence, like that of a man accustomed to choosing his words carefully.

How had he guessed what she'd overheard?

Daniel had conversed with Delilah Fitzwater. Perhaps she had relayed the information to Elliot.

Olivia led Victor to a seating area near a floor-to-ceiling bookcase. His cologne—cedar and spice—filled her nostrils.

She perched on a cushioned chair across from him, rearranging the billowy sleeves of her blouse, then tucking her skirt around her knees.

"I imagine you're curious about what Elliot and I are truly after," Victor continued.

"Enlighten me."

"Elliot and I came to Sweetwater Springs to secure family assets left behind generations ago, legally."

"Ah." She folded her hands in her lap. "Okay."

"I said legally."

"I heard you." She studied him, but his well-practiced charisma exposed nothing. "You mean the power of money brought you here?"

"A sizable trust fund. Also, we're aiming to claim forgotten family bank accounts by proving our relationship."

A contemplative pause hung midair.

"It's not only about finding each other, then," she finally said. "You both have a hidden agenda."

His gaze flitted to the bookshelves. "You make us sound like gold diggers."

"Are you?" As soon as she blurted out the question, she wished she could retrieve the words and return them to the confines of her mouth. She was out of line.

"I prefer to think not. I have a lot of experience in finance." He leaned back. "We're investigating historical bank and property records to find out if a substantial Fitzwater, or Steele family inheritance exists."

Olivia detected a French accent, that was lilting his words, as he elaborated on his intentions.

Her instincts perked. "Forgive my curiosity, but where did you live before coming here?"

"My family moved often when I was young, never settling

down for too long." He turned to the window. "I spent a fair amount of time crisscrossing Europe and the Adriatic coast. Now that I'm here, I rented an apartment near the fountain."

His cultured yet rootless upbringing hinted at a more complex past than merely chasing family fortune. Had boyish dreams once shone in those eyes, clouded by years of roving borders? What youthful ideals or naïve missteps first set him on such a course?

"I couldn't help but notice your limp," she said.

He shrugged. "I had a sports injury when I was young. Soccer. I hoped to have a promising career, but an awkward landing on the field tore a ligament, and my calling ended before it began."

"I'm sorry."

"Don't be. In case you're wondering, I can prove my relation to the Fitzwater lineage." Victor nodded, as if he agreed completely with his own story. "I want my legacy to be officially recognized after being disconnected from relatives for so long."

She smoothed the non-existent wrinkles in her skirt. "How?"

"I have copies of family records—old pedigree charts, faded photographs, generations of Fitzwater heirs." He withdrew a journal from his suit jacket. "My great-grandfather, Algernon Fitzwater, compiled this in the 1920s."

He opened to a page detailing an extensive multibranching lineage tree in faded sepia ink.

"One encircled name near the bottom, Elliot Fitzwater, is connected to a 'Delilah.'"

In his tone, there were deeper currents than merely claiming an old inheritance. Victor had been an outsider, existing on the fraying edges of obscure blood ties. Perhaps he yearned to truly belong somewhere at last and saw taking the Fitzwater name as his path back to roots and legitimacy.

Soon after he left, trailing cigarette smoke behind him, a movement outside caused her to pause.

She exhaled slowly, shaken at the notion of Victor appearing again. This inheritance business unsettled her, but perhaps Daniel could help make sense of it.

She walked to the window, her fingers sliding along the spines of the books lining the shelves. She peered out, anticipation quickening her heartbeat.

A man's silhouette passed by, and her pulse kicked.

Daniel?

No such luck. Besides, he wasn't out of work until six.

It was James McAllister, her former beau.

He extended a friendly wave. "Are you open?" he mouthed.

She sighed and stepped to the counter to stack a last armful of books. "Sure. Why not?"

He greeted her with an overpowering smile as she unlocked the door, and he stepped inside. "Got time to stop by my reopened business? I'd appreciate your magician's eye. Tonight is my unofficial grand opening."

"Tonight?"

"Well, right about now, actually."

His persistent ogling gaze sparked an instinctive response. *Go away, James.*

No doubt Daniel would bristle hearing James sought her company so soon after their meeting by the fountain.

"Ah, goodness, my schedule is completely slammed tonight." She fumbled for a more gracious refusal but couldn't come up with anything.

The shop door opened, and the bell tinkled cheerfully.

Olivia raised her eyes, relieved to see Daniel stride in.

"Afternoon, you two," he greeted easily, though his hard gaze registered James, who was now leaning on the counter. "Or should I say good evening?"

"Daniel, I'm thrilled to see you, as always." Olivia grinned broadly. "James was in the middle of inviting me to check out his latest establishment."

Daniel lifted an eyebrow. "How nice."

"Why don't both of you come and get an exclusive sneak peek?" James straightened. "I'm offering a preview for friends and family before I officially announce my reopening."

With a heavy sigh, Daniel glanced at Olivia. She gave a refined nod. Perhaps this was an ideal opportunity to probe James' impressions of Victor Steele's activities. She assumed their paths might've crossed because Victor's apartment was close to his business.

"We'd love to, James." Olivia twirled a strand of her hair around her finger. "We were hoping to get out and about tonight, weren't we, Daniel?"

"You said you were slammed." James smirked.

"No, no. I got my dates mixed up." Olivia grabbed her cardigan sweater, then locked her bookshop for what she hoped was the last time for the evening. "Lead the way, James!"

As they crossed the street, James detailed his vision for attracting more youthful nightlife crowds. "I wanted to create a space where people can come together, forget their troubles, and have fun." His eyes shimmered with an unmistakable fervor. "Growing up, I found solace in board games. They were my escape from the constant pressure to succeed, to be the perfect son."

Olivia nodded, sensing a deeper story behind his words. She remembered the long hours James spent at his family's stall at the farmer's market, always striving to meet his parents' high expectations.

She offered him a genuine smile. "You're an excellent entrepreneur."

James returned her smile, a flicker of vulnerability

crossing his face. "Thanks, Olivia. That means a lot coming from you."

"This guy never gives up," Daniel whispered to her. "Should I be concerned?"

"You and I are finally together again. Nothing will change that."

His hand slid to the small of her back, his lips grazing her hair. "Right you are, Ollie. I'm here for good."

Seeing him like this, relaxed and smiling, she could hardly believe that this brilliant, sophisticated man who had traveled the world and whom she'd watched on countless television interviews, was the same man who had dreamed with her under a starlit sky.

A few minutes later, the door of *McAllister's Game Haven* swung open.

Mingling scents of piping hot coffee and popcorn hovered in the air, creating an expectant atmosphere.

A vibrant neon sign above the entrance flickered to life, casting an orange glow on the diverse assortment of board games showcased alphabetically by title. Each game, meticulously arranged, waited to be unraveled, offering a realm of strategy and fun. The colorful cardboard boxes promised hours of collaborative quests and laughter-filled nights.

Eager discussions resonated off the exposed brick walls, along with dice rolling and cards shuffling. Background music played too loudly, instrumental video-game soundtracks. An enormous communal table indicated players could gather and try out the games.

At the counter, a knowledgeable and enthusiastic staff member stood ready to shepherd patrons through the extensive selection. He nodded along with the music, as if he totally agreed with every pulsation.

"Best wishes, James." Olivia boosted her voice so it could be heard. "I'm certain this will all be a grand success."

"Thank you." His hand grazed her shoulder, and the contact brought an instinctive clutch to her chest. He lingered too long for friendly comfort as he described the vintage artwork lining the walls.

She slid away to admire the gallery quality *Gone Board Game Girl* lithograph, and James shadowed, gesturing at the brushed steel accents and bold, espresso-colored leather couches by the fireplace.

"With all these nooks for couples, I'm certain business will thrive for sophisticated dates." He gave her a meaningful look, which she avoided by averting her eyes. "Perhaps you'd enjoy trivia night?"

Olivia found Daniel watching this exchange from the bar area with undisguised scrutiny. Their eyes met and his eyebrows pinched together, a silent question as he crossed the room to rejoin her.

Sensing a territorial shift, James pivoted to his grand plans for a gaming tournament. The edge of forced camaraderie lurked beneath their smiles.

"I would be delighted if you shared your ideas for creating a signature cocktail for the lounge," he told Olivia. "I could use a consult on the menu and decor as well."

"And how long might that take?" Daniel interjected, his tone desert dry.

"However long the lady desires." James displayed a roguish grin that Daniel looked ready to peel off with his fists.

She gave Daniel's waist a quick, conciliatory squeeze, and redirected the conversation before flaring tempers ruined their information gathering goals.

"While I'm thinking of it, James, have you seen the guy we were discussing the other day—Victor Steele—lurking around anywhere?" she asked.

"Nope. I can't say I have."

"How about a certain older resident who might come to your shop to while away an afternoon playing board games?"

James arranged a chessboard on a square table and inquired, "What's his name?"

"Clement Aubergine."

"Never heard of the guy," James mumbled, his attention clearly divided between the chess pieces and the conversation.

"Another dead end," Daniel whispered. He exhaled and slid an arm around Olivia's shoulders.

The fringed door curtains parted as laughter mushroomed ahead of an older couple. James' parents, Walter and Harriet McAllister, grinned their greeting as they approached.

"Look who I happened to run into." James gestured to Olivia and Daniel.

Umm, no. James hadn't run into them. He had practically barged into Olivia's bookshop and fairly demanded she attend his "unofficial" opening.

"We wouldn't miss the launch of our son's latest shop for anything!" Harriet reached up to ruffle her son's hair, while Walter grinned behind his thick glasses and clapped James on the back.

As Harriet went on praising her son's clever vision, Olivia found her opportunity when Harriet took a breath.

"James clearly inherited the family's passion for spreading community joy," Olivia said. "Speaking of traditions, did you ever meet a man named Clement Aubergine? He might've lived at the senior facility, but I phoned there, and they've never heard of him. I assume he's in his 70s."

Olivia's search had also extended to archives, employment registries, and real estate—any breadcrumb hinting if Clement resided nearby.

Harriet tapped her lip.

Olivia held her breath.

"The name pings a distant bell." Harriet's eyes briefly glazed over. "What a whirlwind summer back then when he was here. Oh …" Her voice lowered to a murmur.

"Oh?" Olivia tensed—had they crashed into another dead end?

"I'm afraid Clement had a bit of a murky scandal that forced him to leave." Harriet imparted her wisdom uneasily. "Terrible rumors soared about the misfortune—something that happened to his fiancée. Some whispered that he was involved. Nasty business in every direction."

Walter's grin fell away. "Many people turned against Clement after the rumor mill started, and he left and never returned. Can't say I blame him; the whole affair ruined his prospects here."

"Ruined his prospects, how?" Olivia asked.

"A future. A wife."

Olivia mulled over this revelation. Perhaps Clement dated Lillian.

Then again, perhaps she was trying too hard to pin the letter on him. Her mind wandered back to the mystery of the writer, and her growing hunch that Theodore was the key to unlocking the truth.

She dislodged her suspicion and focused on the McAllister couple. "Anything else you might remember?" she asked.

"Clement was a dazzling, nimble-minded fellow." Walter spread his hands wide, adding a touch of theatrics to his description. "He had all the local ladies swooning, with his fancy suits and smooth dance moves."

"And he was chivalrous," Harriet said. "He was constantly opening doors and pulling out chairs for every woman he met."

The man was real, although he'd been gone for decades.

The dazzling Clement didn't live at the senior facility in town. In fact, he'd never lived there. Emma had been wrong, though she'd been speculating, basing her knowledge on hearsay.

Nodding encouragingly, Olivia pressed for more information. "Did anyone stay in contact or have an inkling where Clement might've gone after he left?"

Walter tapped his temple with his forefinger. "Lillian Beaumont sent letters to him for a time. Many folks assumed she got swept up in his orbit along with most of the other ladies."

"Not me," Harriet said.

He smiled. "Not you, my snuggle muffin."

At the stroke of seven, the resonant chime of the clock tower penetrated the walls of the game shop.

"Well, I'll be dipped in gravy! Walter, we forgot to set the DVR for our show." Harriet twisted to Olivia and Daniel. "You two are coming to the potluck, right? It's a cherished tradition, and the sweetheart tree planting is always enchanting. We love to see who is the next to get married. "

Olivia shared a meaningful look at Daniel, remembering Lillian's diary.

"We wouldn't miss either occasion," she said.

As they left James' business, the last traces of daylight had faded, giving way to the glow of the moon. The streetlamps, bright with light, illuminated the sidewalks and storefronts with a dreamlike ambiance, as if Sweetwater Springs had been plucked straight from the pages of a fairytale.

Olivia looped her arm through Daniel's, drawing close to him. He gazed down at her, expressing a depth of longing so intense that she almost forgot to breathe.

She searched his features, his firm lips, and the gravity in those gorgeous eyes, trying to unravel his emotions.

"I'm grateful fate led us back together," she said.

"No one but you could fill the empty space in my life, Ollie. I traveled for years and still felt hollow." He brought his palm to her cheek. "Not anymore."

She burrowed into his shoulder. His hand stroked her hair.

There was no need for words now. All was right in her world.

They passed Mr. Garrison's antique shop on the corner of main and a side street, and Olivia glimpsed a fancy fountain pen in the window display.

"Theodore uses a monogrammed pen like that for his poems," she said. "Often he comes into my bookshop and sits by the corner window and writes and writes." She considered the elaborate cursive script on Lillian's unsigned envelope, visualizing the sweeping artistic embellishments.

"Daniel, wait!" Her voice trembled with excitement. Suddenly, everything clicked into place.

She gulped as memories surged and tapped on the shop's window. "The handwriting on Lillian's letter distinctly matches Theodore's style!"

A thought had always niggled, an insistent tugging. The unique script, with its elongated curves and artistic loops. Where had she seen it before? The answer had hovered and teased, scarcely out of reach.

Until now.

Daniel pressed his face to the window to inspect the pen more closely. "You're thinking our unassuming friend is Lillian's secret admirer?"

"Don't you see? It all adds up. It must be him. Even the nickname Lillian had for him—StormyCuddle."

"I'm not following."

"Newsflash. Theodore's last name is Weatherly. Stormy weather, get it? And cuddle is a cute nickname."

Daniel grinned, a small, satisfied grin.

The truth crystallized like dawn's first light. The quiet poet had been patiently waiting and yearning across the years for this magical ending.

Theodore Weatherly, the Third.

But why had he delayed his reunion with Lillian for so long?

CHAPTER 11

avigating through the rain-kissed streets the next morning, Olivia quickened her pace. The sky, a canvas of muted grays with occasional hints of serene blue, set the stage for another day of ever-changing weather —a tango between brief sunlight and passing showers.

Each of her strides carried purpose, intent on confirming her suspicions about Theodore's hidden love for Lillian.

Butterflies swirled in her stomach as she pushed open the wooden door of *Blissful Bites.* A bell chimed, announcing her arrival.

The scents in the bakery wrapped around her in a comforting hug of sweet temptation, and her mouth watered. Just-out-of-the-oven pastries and steeped coffee shouted promises of indulgence. The warm and inviting aroma of freshly baked bread and cinnamon enveloped her, beckoning from every corner.

It was like a welcome committee for her nose, urging her to leave any calorie concerns at the door and surrender to the scrumptious desserts. A glass counter displayed a colorful array of pastries.

Theodore and Emma sat at a bistro table, chatting over a lavish silver tray—flaky croissants, fruit tarts, and aromatic tea. The gentle clatter of plates and mugs mingled with soft conversation.

"Hi! Pull up a chair!" Emma gestured to Olivia. She set a croissant on her plate and took a bite.

Olivia crossed over to them and added a splash of cream to an empty cup. "You two look comfortable this morning." She studied Emma's face, trying to read any hidden clues. "Are you two catching up on things?"

Theodore gestured to his half-eaten cherry tart and gave a friendly pat to his stomach. "Emma bakes the best tarts in town, carrying on the tradition of her mother and grandmother."

"I second that." Olivia's gaze traced over the twosome, imagining Lillian here with her shy suitor from long ago. The calendar of the past resonated with the heartbeat of the present, and time was turning the page to a final chapter.

Olivia eased into a chair, and poured hot tea, fragrant mint, with a hint of citrus, into her cup. "I've known you quite a while, Theodore, though I was never aware of your prestigious poetry lineage," she began.

He set down his fork. "How did you learn of this?"

"Daniel and I sifted through the town archives at the historical society. Congratulations. You're a poet extraordinaire."

"Thank you." Theodore picked up his cup. "These days, though, writing is a mere hobby, not a pursuit."

"Your signature style remains rather distinct. It's all elongated curves and artistic loops. And you have access to formal stationery."

"Lots of people do,"

"But one of those people is you." She cut right to the

chase. "Are you the person behind the mysterious letter to Lillian?"

Theodore plunged a spoonful of sugar into his tea, then stirred, creating tiny waves. A deliberate dip of his head affirmed her suspicion.

She fixed an encouraging smile on her face. "I should've realized it earlier. Why didn't you tell me right from the start?"

"It's a long story." Emma covered Theodore's hand with her own. "Lillian hails from a wealthy and influential family. The societal expectations assigned to her weren't only about maintaining the Beaumont's standing but also sticking to the norms of an upper-class lineage."

"Right. I understand that." Olivia nodded. "And Theodore?"

"He came from a humble background, known for hard work, although without affluence." Emma shook her head and sighed. "The major social divide. We believe it's in the past, except it never really ends, does it?"

"I disagree. Nowadays, things are different," Olivia said.

Emma shrugged. "If you ask me, economic disparity continues to create barriers."

Olivia let that statement hang in the air and turned to Theodore. "Surely, after all these years, there are no longer any of those obstacles. You're a wealthy man."

"Yes, but fear of rejection runs deep," he replied. "Decades ago, I admired Lillian from a distance. When I finally had my chance, her parents discovered we were seeing each other and sent her away." He lifted a hand. "I hoped she would reach out to me after she left, though she never did. Leading me to believe that she agreed to her mother's demands and no longer wanted to be with me. I'm a wordsmith, but silence can be more powerful. Hers indicated she had moved on."

"You still could've contacted her." Olivia set her cup down firmly, splashing tea over the rim.

"I considered it, often, but her parents made it clear that they disapproved of our relationship. I didn't want to cause any more problems for her."

"You're a good man." Olivia squeezed his hand. "You put her well-being first."

He blinked back the wetness in his eyes and took a shaky breath. "I presumed staying away was the best thing I could do after everything that happened. Her starting over." He gestured vaguely with his other hand. "Away … away from me. I blamed myself and thought she'd be better off."

"She never married."

He exhaled slowly. "Neither did I."

"Never had children."

"Me, neither."

Olivia pursed her lips, pondering her next words. "Here's the thing, Theodore. Why the secrecy? Why not turn the letter over to Lillian when you learned she had returned to Sweetwater Springs and cleared the air?" Frustration crept into her tone even as she tried to soften it with an encouraging half-smile. "It seems a better and more straightforward move."

"Maybe." His eyes narrowed as he gazed out the window at the street. "Our story began at *Harper's Haven* all those years ago."

"Really? *Harper's Haven?*"

"I remember it as if it happened yesterday. Lillian, with her head buried in poetry, and me, rearranging shelves in the bookshop." He leaned back in his chair. "She was striking, and she still is. I've glimpsed her in town several times."

"Have you spoken with her?"

"We waved to each other from across the street."

"Wait, a minute." Olivia's eyes widened as he revealed his

connection. Remarkably, the past had intertwined with the present. "You worked for my grandfather?"

"Yes. Lillian and I spoke nonstop, often losing track of the hours until closing time."

A wave of nostalgia washed over her as she pictured a young Theodore and Lillian, huddled together among the shelves, lost in their shared love of the written word.

She felt a kinship with the pair, understanding the magic of finding a kindred spirit in the pages of a book.

"But why leave the letter for me to discover?" Olivia's fingers traced the floral pattern on the wrought-iron table, searching his conflicted expression for answers.

"An unsigned letter was a discreet way to identify myself, and I knew Lillian would recognize it was me. The bookshop is where we first met." He reached for his fork, carefully dividing a piece of tart, then met Olivia's gaze. "Have you given her the letter yet?"

"I haven't seen her in a couple of weeks."

"Me neither," Emma chimed in.

"She lives alone at the edge of town." Theodore set down his fork. "Suppose something has happened to her."

"Nothing has happened." Emma waved a reassuring hand, though her frown betrayed her creeping doubt. "The Beaumont family employed a caretaker and a housekeeper. I assume Lillian picked up exactly where she left off."

"She was always rather private," Olivia remarked, half to herself. "A few brief sightings around town, but she doesn't dine out much or attend many social events."

Theodore's thick white eyebrows fused together, casting his careworn face in shadow. He eyed Olivia with an intensity that belied his age.

"Please." His voice grew taut, resembling that of a man clinging to a cliff's edge. "Promise me nothing has happened to her."

Olivia withered beneath his imploring gaze. She lifted her teacup, seeking a distraction. How could she guarantee him anything when she hadn't seen Lillian in a while herself?

She took a measured breath. "I'm certain she needs time to readjust to living again in a small town. She was in Tampa for years."

"Yes, but Sweetwater Springs is her hometown."

Olivia offered a smile, faint as fresh spring grass. "People change, and so do their comforts. I'll check on her soon. In the meantime, let her ease into the rhythm of the community on her own terms."

She took out a small notepad and pen from her purse and began jotting notes, organizing her questions. "Why didn't you openly declare your feelings years ago? I'm aware of the societal barriers and all, but still—"

"I believed she understood how much I cared for her. We spent hours together." Theodore began shredding his paper napkin into tiny pieces. "Then, she left. She had to obey her parents, and I lacked the means to pursue her. Plus, she dated a lot of men. In time, I assumed I was merely one of many."

Because he was a humble wordsmith's son. And Lillian, a dazzling socialite's daughter. Their spheres scarcely overlapped except in fleeting moments.

Emma breathed in, a sound that seemed to drain the very air from the room. "Fortunately, fate grants us all second chances."

"Yes." Theodore's eyes glistened. He removed his eyeglasses and pressed the heels of his hands against his closed lids, as if trying to massage away the worry etched into the corners. He composed himself, then placed the glasses back on, signaling his readiness to continue. "When I learned she had returned, every memory of us crowded together. I realized the time had finally come to reveal the contents of my heart."

"Now or never?" Olivia asked.

"Exactly."

"But discreetly."

"Exactly."

"May I ask what's inside the sealed envelope?" Olivia poised a pen over her notebook.

"Whispers of Love." A bittersweet smile crossed his face. "It's a poem I wrote to her many years ago under the willow tree by the pond." His eyes glazed with the varnish of days gone by. "I changed it some after … after everything, but mostly it's the same. Those words carried all the hopes I held for our future together. I'm uncertain if those verses could mend bridges, but I owed it to us to try one last time."

As the importance of his explanation sat between them, Olivia studied the man, her heart breaking for the genuine sorrow and longing haunting him.

She glanced at the door. The bell was quiet, and the space was undisturbed by the usual energy that typically filled Emma's bakery.

"I loved her with every fiber of my being." Theodore's voice wavered as he continued to recount the past. "My own insecurities came between us, and I've carried this regret with me. What might have been if I had only been brave enough to fight for our love?"

Olivia reached across the table, her hand resting on his arm. She understood the years of lost chances that haunted him. "It's not too late," she said. "You'll make things right and share your true feelings. Never allow fear to hold you back."

"Now what about Clement Aubergine?" she prompted, meeting Emma's stare.

"Oh, him." Emma focused on the open front window, where a breeze toyed with the linen curtains. "Once upon a time, he called this town home."

"Yes, decades ago." Olivia set down her pen and notepad, her full attention returning to her companions.

"He pursued Lillian, thinking he could sweep her off her feet with his flashy manners." The edge in Theodore's voice caught Olivia off-guard, and a ghost of a smile crossed his face. "But she saw right through him. Told him flat out that she wasn't interested. He didn't give up easily, though, but then a scandal erupted, and he hightailed it out of town. He's not one to be trusted."

Olivia directed her gaze to Emma. "You had me chasing my tail. You pointed me to Clement to throw me off and spun quite an elaborate yarn."

"I had no choice." Emma straightened a sugar packet and stood. "Theodore swore me to secrecy, and I remember my grandmother mentioning Clement once or twice. He hounded all the ladies."

"I'm glad he's gone," Theodore said.

Emma indulged in a humorous eye roll. "Ever the romantic, this one. I was aware of my deception, but I couldn't break my promise. That's what friends are for."

Olivia wanted to remind them she was their friend too, but she understood their nuanced bond. With Emma's parents gone, Theodore had become a fatherly figure, offering guidance and support beyond friendship.

"I never intended for others to protect me because of my lack of courage." Theodore came to his feet. "I should've trusted my heart rather than hiding my feelings."

Emma went for a tray and stacked their empty cups and plates. "Guarding dreams is never a burden, Theodore. Consider it a blessing." She placed her hand on top of his and tapped a slow, steady rhythm. "Wise men say ..." she sang.

Can't Help Falling in Love by Elvis Presley.

Olivia eyed their bond, appreciative of their devotion to

each other. What firmer foundation existed than when someone accepted you without condition?

She covered their hands, tapping the beat along with Emma.

Perhaps she had done a disservice by imagining them as platonic outsiders, because neither one had a partner.

Fewer relationships ran truer than loyalty.

When Emma finished singing, Olivia reminded Theodore about the rapidly approaching spring potluck supper.

"I'm baking a special cake for the occasion," Emma said.

"I'll bring a batch of my homemade macaroni and cheese," Theodore chimed in. "I hope Lillian is going to be there."

"What will you do? Wave to her from across the room?" Emma teased.

He grinned. "I'll do more than that after Olivia gives her my letter."

Olivia smiled. No matter what, she'd ensure Lillian would attend. Then she'd present her with Theodore's letter in front of the entire town. Two good hearts would find safe harbor after years of wandering in uncertain tides.

"I have a wonderful feeling fate is truly aligning," she said.

The conviction in her voice willed this long-awaited reunion into existence through sheer belief alone.

Theodore managed a small, hopeful smile. "When will you give Lillian my letter?"

"I'll contact her soon."

Only it wouldn't be under the private circumstances he envisioned. The magic of granting his deepest wishes relied on discretion.

With his tender confession still resonating, Olivia realized she hadn't mentioned the engraved letters in the hidden gazebo.

"StormyCuddle." She paused. "I saw that in the gazebo."

A flush of color crept into Theodore's cheeks, adding a

touch of vulnerability to his otherwise composed demeanor, revealing the youthful spirit lingering inside. "Lillian's nickname for me. I'm surprised the words are still there."

"They are."

"Sometimes, it seems like a lifetime ago. Other times, it's as if it happened yesterday." He chuckled, his gaze fixed on the rolling pin hanging on the wall, Emma's attempt at decorating. "Lillian and I were a couple of adventurous kids with lofty ambitions. The gazebo held a special significance for us. We expressed many wishes there under the night sky."

Daniel and I confided in each other at night, too, Olivia thought.

Theodore's lips twitched into a sideways grin. "Carving the nickname was my brilliant idea. We were goofing around, talking about the future. I took out my pocket knife and tried not to mess it up. 'StormyCuddle' felt right, you know?"

"It still feels right," Olivia assured. Resting her chin in her hand, she pictured a gangly teenage Theodore trying to hide his nerves as he etched this pet name in the gazebo woodwork. They were youthful, hopeful, and blissfully unaware of the painful circumstances that would keep them apart.

She felt a pang of sympathy for the unassuming man, realizing that beneath his quiet exterior lay a heart full of desire and disappointment. How many years had he carried this burden, never sharing his true feelings? Her admiration for him grew, and she silently vowed to do everything in her power to help him reconnect with his lost love.

"You both shared something incredibly special." Olivia blinked back tears. "Something real and lasting. It's time to mend the last threads."

"Funny how a simple carving can turn into a story." He gave a small shrug, as if trying to downplay the sentimentality of it all. Nonetheless, the gleam in his blue eyes spoke more than a thousand words. He still loved Lillian very much.

As Olivia formulated her plan to surprise Lillian with Theodore's letter at the potluck, a twinge of guilt tugged. Theodore had entrusted her with his deepest feelings, expecting her to deliver the message privately.

But something in her heart told her that this moment deserved to be shared with the entire town, a celebration of love's enduring power. She wrestled with the decision, weighing his trust against the potential for a truly enchanted reunion. In the end, her belief in the life-changing influence of love won out, and she silently prayed that he would understand and forgive her for the public revelation.

As she left *Blissful Bites*, her mind buzzed. His revelations had only strengthened her resolve.

With a determined stride, she stepped back to her book-shop, the fresh breeze carrying the scent of blossoming flowers and the promise of new beginnings.

THE NEXT AFTERNOON, Olivia retraced her steps to the secluded gazebo.

Her heart raced in expectation. Her decision wasn't rational, but intuitive, and she had placed a 'Closed Out to Lunch' sign on her bookshop's door. She rationalized that she would only be gone a short time.

There was more to discover. She just knew it. Perhaps a sigh in the breeze or a fleeting image from her last visit with Daniel had stirred her.

Before long, she stood before the gazebo, its weathered wood and intricate carvings holding the secrets of countless memories. She took a deep breath, steeling herself for what she might uncover, and stepped inside.

She crouched down, the rich scent of soil filling her nostrils. She slipped on her gloves and brushed away the dirt.

A glimmer caught her eye—the same glimmer she remembered from the other day. A gold locket lay nestled in the earth like a long-buried secret, waiting to be brought to light. Carefully, she extracted the locket, its surface covered in a greenish patina.

The cool metal seemed to pulse, the delicate chain whispering as it slipped through her fingers. As she cradled it in her palm, she marveled at the intricate engravings, the grooves and curves telling a story of their own.

She opened it, revealing a miniature tableau and several hidden pockets. In one, she discovered two intertwined initials: L.B. and C.A.

Lillian Beaumont and …

And who?

The realization struck her like a thunderbolt, and she stared at the locket in her trembling hands. Could C.A. be the initials of Clement Aubergine? Had he and Lillian shared a secret rendezvous at this very gazebo? Olivia's mind reeled with the implications, questioning if she had underestimated the capricious, fickle nature of teenage romance.

She cringed at the potential consequences. The last thing she wanted was to ignite the flames of jealousy and stir up a long-buried love triangle. She found herself torn between divulging this discovery and protecting the gentle, unsuspecting Theodore.

Her heart ached. His dreams would shatter.

She closed her eyes, trying to make sense of the conflicting emotions that swirled within her. Despite her desire to safeguard Theodore from potential heartbreak, she recognized that the truth, regardless of its discomfort, had to be brought to light. With a deep breath, she steeled herself for the difficult conversation that lay ahead.

She sat on the bench, the locket heavy in her hands.

For several minutes, she struggled with her conscience, debating the best course of action. Should she confront Lillian privately, giving her a chance to explain her past with Clement? Or should she go directly to Theodore, risking his trust by revealing this new information?

A half hour later, she barely registered the hurried footsteps approaching from behind until Daniel came into view.

"Sorry, I got tied up at the historical society," he said, slightly out of breath.

She tilted her head. "Doing what?"

"Making phone calls. I might have to return to London for a brief spell."

He hadn't mentioned the limestone tablet and the British Museum, and she was at a loss for how to broach the subject. So, she remained silent, and so did he.

"Is there a reason you wanted to meet here again?" he continued. "I don't mean to rush you, but I'm pressed for time."

"I found something disturbing that might change everything."

She handed him the locket.

His brow furrowed. "What is this? Where did you find it?"

"Here. Where Theodore and Lillian met. Look inside, at the initials."

He pried open the locket, pausing before reading the inscription aloud. "L.B. and C.A.? Could this be …?"

"Clement Aubergine," Olivia confirmed. "Lillian may have been involved with him, even while she was seeing Theodore."

Daniel was silent for a long moment. "This might ruin everything," he finally said. "If Theodore finds out …"

"We can't keep it from him. He deserves to have full knowledge of the truth, no matter how much it hurts."

Daniel turned the locket, catching the sunbeam's rays as he examined it further. "Hold on, let's not assume the worst. Check closer." He traced the faint engraving. "These initials are D.F."

"They are?" Olivia's voice was barely a whisper.

"The shape of the letters is similar, but definitely D.F."

"Delilah Fitzwater? The matchmaker who never married?"

"Possibly."

"She was seeing Clement Aubergine?"

"Why not?" Daniel handed the locket back to her. "He charmed most of the ladies in town."

Laughter bubbled up from Olivia, dispelling the tension. "I'm beyond relieved."

The distant sound of children playing drifted in the air, a reminder of the carefree innocence that once characterized Theodore and Lillian's adolescent love.

With a shaky breath, she closed her fingers around the locket, holding it close. She silently vowed to do everything in her power to bring them back together and help them reclaim the affection they had been denied for so long. It was more than just a romantic notion; it was a sacred mission, a chance to heal old wounds and prove that true love conquered all.

With this admission, the path seemed clear. At the upcoming potluck supper, two fated souls would finally reunite.

CHAPTER 12

*T*he following afternoon, Olivia hesitated only a moment before punching in Lillian's phone number to extend a personal invitation to the potluck supper. This pivotal gesture would ensure the secret star guest appeared for her long-awaited romantic reunion.

Lillian answered on the third ring, her refined voice instantly recognizable. "Why, Olivia, darling! This is a delight. I was thinking of you recently, and I'm overdue for a visit to your bookshop."

Olivia was relieved that Lillian was okay. "I haven't seen you around a lot these last few weeks," she said.

"Oh, I was fighting a cold, but I feel much better. Barring a relapse, I should be fine for the event."

As they exchanged cordial pleasantries, Olivia marveled inwardly at how Lillian sounded precisely the sophisticated, ageless woman that she was, save for a subtle, weary undertone etching the cheerful façade. Would her recent illness have etched faint lines around the impeccable socialite's sparkling green eyes?

Nevertheless, Lillian acknowledged attending the potluck

event. "I look forward to seeing friendly faces, and I'll bring the traditional Beaumont family salad."

"I've heard all about it," Olivia replied. "My grandfather mentioned it time and again. Your secret is toasted hazelnuts and thinly sliced radishes."

She'd also read about the dish in Lillian's diary, but she kept that knowledge to herself.

"And goat cheese. The hazelnuts are from Oregon." While Lillian spoke, Olivia nodded along, mentally envisioning the ingredients.

After finalizing the call, she breathed easier. The guest list blessedly confirmed Lillian's attendance. As for Olivia, she'd contribute her own family's traditional recipe—deviled eggs with a new twist—flavored with smoked paprika.

LATER THE FOLLOWING WEEK, Olivia locked the bright-red door of her bookshop for the evening, anticipating Daniel's arrival home from London. She pulled her olive-green wool coat tighter against the night's chill. Underneath, she wore a cream lace blouse tucked into a long floral cotton skirt that swished around her calves as she walked. Her chestnut waves were styled into a loose ponytail, secured with a velvet bow.

Daniel came around the corner, his familiar rugged features illuminated by the golden glow of the streetlamps. His deep brown hair curled slightly over his forehead, while his jaw boasted a hint of a dark stubble, a persistent five o'clock shadow no matter the time of day. He wore jeans, boots, and a brown leather jacket over an untucked white button-down shirt. As he drew Olivia into a heartfelt embrace, his hazel eyes glinted with affection.

She nestled into his chest and breathed in the clean, cotton and invigorating spring air that encircled him.

"Ollie, I've missed you a lot these last few busy days," he said.

"I've missed you, as well." So much that sometimes she couldn't breathe for missing him and waiting for his phone call, yearning to hear his voice. He'd only managed to call her once, and their conversation was brief.

He slung an arm around her shoulders. "What do you say to a sunset chat while I walk you home?"

"Sure." She nodded, though her relief at his return was overshadowed by many unanswered questions.

They strolled down cobblestone lanes toward her apartment on Mistwood Lane. On the way, she recounted her pivotal confrontation with Theodore and Emma, where Theodore finally admitted his feelings for Lillian.

During their last meeting, she hadn't gotten the chance to tell him the entire story because the discovery of the locket took over and he'd left in a hurry. Walking together side by side, this conversation became a cathartic release, and her words flowed freely.

She described every detail in Emma's bakery, from the tremor in Theodore's voice to the shimmering tears in his eyes, painting a picture of a love that had endured the test of time.

Daniel listened attentively, grinning, silently supporting.

"Our poet laureate was truly the mystery man pining for lovely Lillian," she went on. "He intentionally misled us by joining our search for a man in a fedora at the fountain. There he was, right in front of us, reciting poetry and displaying postcards, although he concealed his secret."

Daniel's grin persisted. "Quite a shock, yet it makes perfect sense. Literature and sonnets were their first bond in your grandfather's bookshop. So, what's next?"

"I intend to hand deliver Theodore's letter to Lillian at the potluck supper."

"Does he know your plan?"

"He knows he's attending. He has persistently inquired about the letter, though I've managed to evade his queries.

"And Lillian?"

"I finally caught up with her by phone. She's attending, too, and offered to bring a salad." Olivia gave Daniel a teasing elbow. "Exactly like her family did in years gone by."

"Followed by Lillian and Theodore planting a sweetheart tree together?"

"That's the plan. Hopefully, resulting in a wedding."

As they continued, Olivia detailed her matchmaking scheme. When the conversation lulled, a flicker of concern crept into her heart. Despite the comfort of Daniel's presence, the unresolved legal troubles he faced abroad weighed heavily on her mind.

Her steps slowed as she turned to face him. "We've been focused on Theodore and Lillian. However, I'm concerned about your situation. Have there been any updates on the law-related issues you're dealing with?"

His grin faded. He avoided her gaze and offered his usual vague reassurances.

This time, she refused to let the matter drop. She confronted him about his pattern of disappearing abroad whenever she asked too many questions.

"I've only been gone twice in two weeks, Ollie." He ran his fingers through his hair, disheveling the dark strands, the image of conflict wrestling with competing priorities. "Just twice."

While that was true, these weren't quick errands to the local grocery store. He had flown to England, and his explanations were invariably evasive.

Her mind circled back to the possibility that he was taking covert emergency measures related to the overseas shipment scandal. Had he truly cut ties with his global treasure hunting networks, which seemed to operate in ethical gray areas? Had the authorities been appeased without imposing any penalties?

Her heart sank, though she stood her ground. "Trust requires honesty, Daniel. Let me help you, or …"

"Or what?"

She took a deep breath, steeling herself for what she needed to say. "Or … or maybe we should end our relationship. I've had enough secrets lately to last me a lifetime."

"Ollie, I can handle this without your help." He brushed her off with a brief parting kiss as they reached her apartment.

"That's it?" she asked.

"For now, yes."

The truth of where she stood in his priorities shone painfully clear, and honesty was obviously nonexistent.

She retreated into her empty foyer, the cold night closing in around her. A growing distance hung between them, and the uncertainty of their future pressed on her heart.

THE MORNING of the potluck supper, Olivia sorted through decorations at the historical society hall, mentally checking off the preparation list.

She'd seen Daniel, because he worked there, and the atmosphere between them was tense. In the wake of their recent argument, they studiously avoided each other and rarely spoke.

Talk about awkward, although she couldn't dwell on it.

Antique lanterns … check. Flower garlands … check. She wanted the setting to be perfect.

As she untangled a string of lights, the door creaked open. "Don't mind me dropping in," came a familiar voice that made her pulse involuntarily stop.

James sauntered toward her, his roguish grin in place.

"James!" She stepped back. "What a surprise. Can I … help you with something?"

He sidled up to her. "I was passing by and saw you through the window. Clearly, you need my assistance." Before she could decline, he reached for the lights in her hand. "Here, let me hang those for you."

Intent on playing would-be hero, he dragged over a ladder despite an earlier pronouncement that maintenance wasn't his strong suit. When Olivia checked her watch, realizing Daniel might come by at any moment, James waved off her concern, evidently reading her mind.

"Your boyfriend gets irrationally jealous. Why stress him when you've got me here?" He grabbed a hammer and nails, winking as he positioned the ladder against the wall. They stood shoulder-to-shoulder.

"Hold the ladder for me, beautiful?" he asked, prompting her assistance.

Daniel entered the hall, and she groaned inwardly. His smile instantly cooled several degrees as he noticed James, her persistent admirer.

"Well, isn't this cozy … again." he announced with barbed emphasis.

Olivia called out to enlist the help of Delilah and Nora. They were arranging pastel pink and purple streamers, decorating every spare corner.

"Ladies, can you give James a hand?" Olivia shouted.

"I'm happy to oblige," Delilah said as both ladies stepped over.

"How is Victor?" Olivia asked, knowing that Elliot had introduced Victor to Delilah.

"Victor left abruptly. He's an odd sort, but I'm glad to learn he's family."

"And Elliot?"

"He moved in with me and is doing his Elliot thing. He mentioned something about a sizable trust fund and forgotten bank accounts. Nothing has come to fruition, so he's looking for a job. And, because of me, he's dating …" She pointed toward Nora, apparently keen to play matchmaker anew. "Ooh, it reminds me of my younger days."

"Wonderful news!" Olivia said.

"I think so, too." Nora chuckled, her eyes perceptive behind horn-rimmed spectacles, as she steadied the ladder for James.

Theodore and Emma entered the hall, carrying an enormous cake on a white pedestal. The cake featured layers of handcrafted sugar flowers—daisies and tulips—and was decorated with fresh strawberries.

The cake became a focal point, sparking conversations and admiration about Emma's latest creation.

"Olivia." Emma paused. "Who was that good-looking guy who stopped by your bookshop the other day? Dark hair … mysterious."

"Victor Steele?" Olivia blinked. "Apparently, he's related to Elliot. Why?"

"Just asking." Emma shrugged and turned to Theodore as they placed the cake in the center of the dessert table. "Thank you for helping me. What would I do without you?"

"Any time." Theodore blushed and Olivia smiled.

If only he knew what was in store for him. Love always found its rightful home, and Sweetwater Springs stood ready to witness a fairytale reawakened.

She surveyed the transformed space.

"Daniel, this night is going to be magical." She turned, eager to share her excitement with him, to see the same hope and happiness reflected in his eyes. But as she scanned the room, her smile faltered. He was nowhere to be seen.

Despite their disagreement, she had assumed he would be

by her side, supporting her through this emotional journey, just like he had been from the beginning. His absence felt like a physical ache, a hollow space where his reassuring presence should have been.

She took a deep breath, trying to push down the rising sense of disappointment. Perhaps he had stepped away for a moment, caught up in some last-minute detail or conversation. He knew how much this event meant to her, how invested she was in seeing Theodore and Lillian's love story come full circle.

Though as the minutes ticked by, her sadness grew. She scanned the crowd, searching for his familiar smile, those warm eyes that always steadied her.

How could he disappear so quickly? Was he having second thoughts about their relationship, doubts about their future together? Or had he been torn away by his complicated life?

Whatever the reason, his absence left a bitter taste in her mouth, a nagging sense of disappointment that threatened to overshadow the happiness of the evening. She had counted on him to be her rock, her partner in this emotional endeavor. And now, she felt strangely alone.

Sure, they hadn't resolved their disagreement from the other day. But still …

Olivia squared her shoulders, determined not to allow his disappearance to ruin this special night. She had worked too hard, poured too much of her heart into bringing Theodore and Lillian together. But even as she pasted on a smile for Delilah, Nora, and even for James, she couldn't shake the sense that something precious had slipped away exactly when she needed it most.

. . .

IN THE EARLY AFTERNOON, Olivia stood before the mirror in her apartment, scrutinizing her reflection as she put the final touches on her appearance. She styled her chestnut brown hair, which fell past her shoulders in shiny, loose curls to frame her face, and opted for a side part.

She chose a knee-length dress featuring a modest neckline and cinched waist. The cotton fabric whispered against her skin, and the subtle floral scent of her perfume enveloped her in a cloud of femininity. She pulled on a pair of mismatched socks, and sturdy ankle boots.

To add a dash of classic glamour, she pinned back a few strands of hair with a silver hair clip set with a tiny, glistening pearl. The cool metal contrasted with the warmth of her chestnut curls. Her grandmother's pearls around her neck added the final touch.

She skillfully applied a thin line of dark brown eyeliner along her upper lashes, winging it out slightly at the outer corners for a cat-eye effect. Two coats of black mascara emphasized the depth of her dark eyes. To complete the look, she used a creamy lipstick in a dusty rose shade that complemented her complexion.

She tucked Theodore's letter into her tote bag, then did one final check by phone to ensure that all the key players would be in attendance for the big surprise reunion.

Everyone assured her that they would be there … everyone, that is, except Lillian, who cited a bothersome headache.

"The last remnants of my cold," she said. "I'll try to make an appearance later if it fades."

Olivia's buoyant mood sank like a stone. Could all this be ripped away by a headache?

She hesitated about calling Daniel, and decided that if he wanted to find her, he knew where to look. He'd once declared the historical society his second home, and that's where she would be.

Fraught with tension, half doubtful Lillian wouldn't attend, Olivia chose not to upset Theodore with last-minute reservations. She'd trust destiny and true love to win the day.

One last worry, and she pushed it out of her mind.

What if Lillian's affection for Theodore had indeed been fleeting? Then all the town would witness Theodore's embarrassment and heartache.

CHAPTER 13

*W*ith two dozen deviled eggs packed in a cooler, Olivia drove the short distance to the historical society building and parked outside. She set the eggs on a long side table, then scanned the hall. A small podium stood at one end.

In each corner, old-fashioned barrels overflowed with daffodils and tulips in mason jars, freshly picked from local gardens, adding a touch of natural beauty to the space. Rustic linens draped the tables, and centerpieces crafted from repurposed driftwood, moss, and wildflowers decorated them, echoing the stunning magnificence of the surrounding landscape.

Townspeople soon filtered in, exchanging laughter and greetings.

Theodore looked exceedingly handsome in khaki trousers, slightly creased, paired with a button-up shirt in light blue. Over the shirt, he wore a lightweight knit sweater. A polka-dotted bow tie made him stand out with a dash of old-world charm.

He opened the lid of his covered container, macaroni and

cheese, and the irresistible aroma of melted cheese filled the air.

Emma walked behind him. With her penchant for stylish clothes, she'd opted for a jumpsuit with a cinched waist and wide-legged pants. The forest-green color accented her fair skin and rosy cheeks. Her naturally wavy blond hair added a touch of whimsy to her overall appearance, softening the tailored lines.

Nora, wearing a floral red dress, entered on Elliot's arm, with a beaming Delilah behind them. Nora brought a home-made chicken and vegetable stew, and the aroma of herbs and spices wafted from the pot.

"This was a joint effort, sugar plum." Delilah hip-bumped Nora. "I chopped the vegetables, and Nora supplied the thyme from her own herb garden."

Olivia laughed and thanked them. She stepped to the buffet table, and arranged silverware, plates, and napkins.

She looked around. There was no sign of Lillian.

Or Daniel, for that matter. He'd obviously opted to skip the event.

The McAllister couple contributed a delectable beef dish, and Mrs. McAllister declared that she'd slow-cooked the meal to perfection. She also made her excuses for James, who couldn't attend because his game shop was open and thriving.

The aroma of the various dishes combined with the buttery, enticing scent of freshly baked rolls, and the tanta-lizing sweetness of Emma's cake. The room buzzed, the clinking of dinnerware and cutlery providing a cheery back-drop to the festivities.

In the center of each table stood a tall, slender vase, teeming with the delicate blossoms of cherry trees and forsythia branches. These branches reached upwards, creating an ethereal canopy of pale pink and golden-yellow.

Antique lanterns hung from wooden beams, casting an amber glow reminiscent of flickering gaslights from the past.

Theodore glanced around, obviously looking for Lillian, though he was apparently trying to play it cool.

Olivia sat at various tables, immersed in the collective memories and heartfelt connections shared among the guests. The hall overflowed with chuckles, nostalgic tales, and the clinking of glasses as old friends reminisced, and new ties were forged. Snippets of conversation drifted—tales of childhood adventures and the triumphs and trials that had shaped their lives.

Olivia listened to their stories, offering a comforting touch or a knowing smile when emotions ran high. However, as the main course drew to a close and the townspeople cleared away the bowls, she couldn't shake off her sadness.

She had meticulously planned every detail. Yet, as she surveyed the hall, the much-anticipated reunion had not materialized. Theodore sat quietly in a corner, his eyes often darting toward the entrance, and Lillian was nowhere to be seen.

As Olivia gathered more empty plates, her mind was clouded with doubts.

She busied herself with preparing the dessert table and thought of Daniel. His absence had been obvious throughout the evening, and she missed him. Just as she was about to lose herself in a spiral of melancholy, footsteps echoed behind her.

"I'm sorry I'm late." Daniel's voice cut through the air, causing her to spin around. He strode toward her, a stack of store-bought cookies in his hands and a sheepish grin on his face. The cookie assortment included an eclectic mix of flavors—from classic chocolate chip to decadent double fudge. "I had matters to clear up."

"What kind of matters?" she asked.

"Matters that don't matter anymore." Mischief danced in his hazel eyes, a glint of sincerity mingling in the depths. Olivia's heart quickened, a flutter resonating with their unspoken connection.

"Here is my cookie contribution," he said.

Unable to contain herself, Olivia burst into laughter, the tension of the evening momentarily forgotten. "This is the Tower of Temptation?" She gestured toward the precariously stacked cookies.

"Go ahead! Try to resist," he teased. "I may not be a chef, but I've mastered the art of cookie selection.

"Then you're on time. I was preparing to serve dessert."

As they arranged the table, their earlier tension faded. The familiar rhythm of their movements and the brushing of their hands as they reached for cups and saucers rekindled the love that had always existed between them.

However, she searched his face for answers to the questions that plagued her, and uncertainty still flickered in the pit of her stomach. She loved him with all her heart, but a tiny voice in the back of her mind whispered, "What if he leaves again? What if the allure of adventure proves too strong?" She tried to push the thought away, focusing on the happiness of the moment, but the seeds of doubt lingered, waiting to take root.

"Daniel," she began, her tone barely audible above the chatter of the guests. "Where did you go once you arrived in England? What happened?"

He stiffened, as if steeling himself for the conversation.

"Ollie, I owe you an explanation." He followed her into the kitchen and set the cookies on the counter. "I didn't want to burden you with the troubles I've been facing."

"But I knew already. I heard it firsthand, and I wanted to help."

"The disappearance of the limestone tablet caused a great

deal of turmoil for me and my former colleagues. The ethical and professional implications are enormous if anything goes wrong." He breathed in, then slowly exhaled. "I'm a researcher. I'm expected to act professionally."

"You did," she replied.

"I tried, but if I lost a valuable piece, the loss could be seen as a breach of contract. It would have affected my credibility and standing in the academic community. And worse, the authorities might have taken legal action if foul play was suspected. I could've been tied up in the court system for months, or even years. I would never have put you through that."

She could hardly imagine the extent of the complications he had been grappling with. Inwardly, she processed the enormity of his statement.

"You've been through so much," she said.

"This morning," he continued, "I received word that they found the tablet. That's why I left the hall so quickly. I have been cleared of any wrongdoing, and the matter is resolved once and for all."

The knots in her stomach unraveled. "So, what does this mean for you?"

"It means that I have officially concluded my former job. And I realize that I should have leaned on you during my difficult time. Please accept my apology for shutting you out." He took her hands in his. "I'm ready to leave that life behind and start here in Sweetwater Springs, with you. I'm sorry."

"You already apologized."

"I'm saying it again." A smile slowly spread across his face. "I should have been fully transparent, but I wanted to protect you. Do you know why?"

Tears of relief pricked at the corners of her eyes. "Why?"

"Because I love you, Ollie, and I've vowed to safeguard you against anything that might hurt you."

"You left me once. That hurt."

"Never again. I've always loved you."

"I wasn't certain …"

"No more secrets, no more disappearances." His arms encircled her waist. "But I have a question."

"What is it?"

"Do you like chocolate chip cookies?"

She detected a gleam of mischief in his eyes.

"What? You know I do."

He acknowledged the stack of cookies with a nod, then pulled a small, square-shaped box from his pocket and set it on the topmost cookie.

"This is for you," he said softly.

"I'm your top cookie," she teased.

"Of course. But there's more." He handed her the box. "This is for you, too."

She opened the hinged lid. Inside, a magnificent diamond ring rested on a black velvet lining, glittering, and scattering rainbow fragments across the kitchen.

She gave a silent nod because she couldn't utter anything that resembled a sound.

He dropped to one knee. "I've imagined this moment countless times … rehearsed what I would say."

"Daniel …"

"No, please. Let me finish." He swallowed. "Your kindness won my heart years ago. You've been my anchor, and I want to spend the rest of my life by your side."

Olivia felt the sting of joyful tears, the salt mingling with the sweetness of this moment on her tongue.

"Will you marry me?" he asked.

"Yes. Yes, yes."

"I love you, Ollie Harper. I've always loved you."

"And I love you, Daniel Whitfield." She caught an inscription on the inside of the ring band and stared at it for several seconds.

One word.

Jackpot.

Her throat constricted. She tried to smile, to laugh. "Does this cookie have lots of chocolate chips?" she joked, wondering if he'd remember.

"Loaded."

He remembered.

He slid the ring on her finger, stood, and wrapped her in his arms.

The disappointment of the evening's unrealized surprise faded into the background. The true miracle lay in the love that she and Daniel had forged, a bond that emerged stronger than ever.

With renewed optimism, she turned her attention back to the dessert table. The potluck supper may not have unfolded exactly as she had envisioned, but the most important pieces of her life had fallen into place.

With a sigh, she decided to sit with Theodore for a while.

Suddenly, the doors of the hall opened once more, and there stood Lillian, radiant as ever, wearing her signature red lipstick.

She glided into the room, her presence commanding attention, and immediately drew awed whispers. Despite the silver in her impeccably coiffed hair and the delicate lines etched on her face, she radiated a timeless grace. Her piercing green eyes, reminiscent of an enchanted forest, sparkled with the wisdom of a life well lived. Draped in a red silk blouse adorned with a lustrous white gold necklace, a black pencil skirt, and a stunning pair of earrings, she was the epitome of sophistication.

On seeing her, Olivia's relief was so intense that it nearly took her breath away.

She glanced at Theodore.

His face transformed, shock giving way to pure delight, and she knew that all her efforts had been worth it. His gaze found Lillian's, and decades of desire passed between them.

Olivia smiled. She had played a part in bringing these two together, in reigniting a love that had never truly died. And that was a gift beyond measure.

"Lillian! I'm so glad you're here!" She rushed over to greet her, catching the scent of Lillian's perfume. The fragrance was rich and complex, with notes of sandalwood and vanilla surrounding her.

"I told you I would attend if I felt better, and I apologize for my lateness. Everyone has already eaten, but I brought a spring salad." Lillian handed Olivia a large glass trifle bowl. "The grocer was out of butter lettuce, so I used baby spinach instead. The strawberries are ripe, and very sweet." Her hands, perfectly manicured, betrayed no signs of age, a testament to her meticulous self-care.

"Your salad looks delicious." Olivia admired the intricate etchings on the bowl and set the salad on a table. "Thank you. I have no problem eating vegetables with dessert, and I'm sure all the guests will agree."

She made eye contact with Theodore, then reached for his envelope in her tote bag.

He shook his head. "No," he said quietly.

"Why not?" Daniel walked up to Theodore. "Here's your chance," he said, in a voice loud enough for everyone in the hall to hear. "Don't let fear hold you back. You owe it to yourself, and to her."

Theodore nodded, reluctantly at first, then more vigorously.

He understood. Now or never.

Olivia's heart drummed a rhythm of nerves and excitement as she stepped to the podium. Clearing her throat to command attention, she tapped the side of a glass.

As the room fell silent and all eyes turned toward her, she held up Theodore's envelope for all to see, then encouraged him to come forward.

His gaze locked with Lillian's, his expression revealing a powerful emotion that sent shivers down Olivia's spine. With measured steps, he made his way to the podium.

"Do you have a message to convey, Theodore?" Olivia asked, handing him the envelope.

"I do, as a matter of fact," he replied, his voice shaky. "Something that I've cherished in my soul for decades. This is a poem I wrote for Lillian Beaumont many years ago."

Taking a seat near the podium, Lillian stared at him, her hand finding its place over her heart.

His eyes never left hers. He opened the envelope and extracted a worn piece of paper. In a tone filled with devotion and yearning, he began,

"In whispers soft, my heart does speak,
Of love that spans both strong and meek.
For years on end, my soul did yearn,
For thee, my love, for thee I yearn.
From humble roots, my life did bloom,
Yet in your gaze, my world finds room.
Though wealth and status set us apart,
In love's embrace, we share one heart.
Though time may steal our youthful glow,
Our love, like rivers, still does flow.
With every breath, with every sigh,
Our love endures, it will not die.
Whispers of love, for all to hear,
A testament to what is dear.
For in your arms, I've found my home,

With you, my love, I'll never roam."

Few guests comprehended the gravity of the poem—though his public outpouring unlocked a hidden world.

Lillian's eyes grew wide, like a woman grasping a much-awaited second chance.

He stepped up to her and pressed the envelope into her open palm.

"Lillian, my sweetheart, I've carried these feelings in my heart forever and a day, waiting and wondering. I loved you when we were in our teens, and I love you now. Tomorrow, I'll love you even more."

A cry escaped Lillian's throat, and she flung her arms around him. "I love you, Theodore. I've always loved you."

Tears streamed down both their faces.

Olivia swallowed hard. Pride, elation, and fulfillment swelled within her, and she blinked back tears of her own.

She glanced at Daniel as he approached, and she recognized the same emotion reflected in his eyes. This was what true love looked like—a pledge that withstood the test of time.

As friends surrounded Theodore and Lillian, offering congratulations and good wishes, Olivia leaned into Daniel's embrace.

"How does the saying go?" he mused. "All's well that ends well."

She grinned. "They're proving it's never too late for a sweet ending."

His lips brushed her cheek. "And our story is just getting started."

She marveled at the strange workings of fate, at how it had united Theodore and Lillian. It was as if the long, lonely winter of their separation had finally given way to the warm, gentle rains of spring, nurturing the seeds of their love, and allowing them to bloom once more.

An hour later, when the last guests filtered out of the hall, Olivia and Daniel walked to the park. Once there, she gazed at the emerging stars.

The doubts that lingered in the back of her mind resurfaced. She turned to him, her gaze searching his.

"I need to be certain … are you really here to stay?" She glanced at the diamond ring on her finger. "I love you so much, but I'm scared. Scared that you'll leave, that the call of adventure will be too strong for you to resist."

"Ollie, you are my greatest adventure." He pressed his forehead against her hair. "Loving you is the most important aspect of my life. I nearly lost sight of that once. I'll never lose sight of it again."

He cuddled her, the warmth of his body shielding her from the cool night air. The soft chirping of crickets and the distant hooting of an owl created a soothing melody, a perfect accompaniment to the intimacy of the moment. His fingers drew light patterns on her back, igniting sparks of love that danced beneath her skin.

He nodded toward Theodore and Lillian, who cradled a fragile sapling.

A cherry blossom tree.

Two holes for planting had already been dug.

"Ollie, will you join me in this tradition?" Daniel asked, hesitating, waiting for her response. He gestured to a second sapling.

Olivia smiled. "Nothing would make me happier."

Their own love was taking its first tender roots.

They kneeled beside Theodore and Lillian and nestled their saplings into the earth. There were no flowers yet. It would take a few years.

The breeze, like a mischievous accomplice, carried their laughter through the grove. The saplings appeared relatively small compared to the mature trees, with slender trunks, sparse branches, and foliage that was still developing.

Nonetheless, they were a symbol of love's enduring strength.

Their hands brushed as they patted the soil, and Olivia realized a profound connection—to the earth, to the ticking of time, and to the man beside her.

She regarded Theodore and Lillian, their faces impressed by happiness, and a realization dawned.

This ceremony—this act of planting and nurturing—was a beautiful metaphor for love itself. Just as the saplings needed care, attention, and years to flourish, so too did a relationship. It required patience, dedication, and a willingness to trust.

With each passing season, the roots would expand, and the branches would thrive. This was the promise of a future.

She was ready to plant the seeds of their romance and watch it flourish, day by day, season by season.

"Ollie?" He whispered something in her ear.

She glanced up at him. "What did you say?"

He leaned closer, speaking in whispers.

Whispers of love.

EPILOGUE

ne year later …

As the golden light of a late April afternoon filtered through the lace curtains of *Harper's Haven*, Olivia snuggled in a leather armchair in her bookshop, a worn album resting on her lap. Her beloved grandfather had passed the album, filled with sepia-toned photographs and cherished memories, down to her.

Her fingers outlined the faces of her grandparents, Elijah and Rachel, as they smiled up at her from the faded photographs. She could almost hear their voices, overflowing with wisdom, guiding her through the incredible journey she had experienced over the past year in Sweetwater Springs.

Her grandfather's influence lived on in each corner of *Harper's Haven*, from the carefully curated shelves to the inviting ambiance that greeted readers of all ages. Olivia recalled the countless hours she spent by his side, learning the intricacies of running a bookshop, and the thrill of connecting with customers through a shared appreciation for literature. And her grandmother Rachel's spirit was intricately woven into the very fabric of Olivia's life, from the pearl necklace gracing her neck to the cherished recipe for deviled eggs, a beloved staple at every Sweetwater Springs gathering.

As Olivia turned the pages, her mind wandered back to the past year. She had evolved, both personally and professionally. The challenges of running the book shop taught her resilience, adaptability, and the importance of staying true to her grandfather's legacy. Her confidence in her abilities had grown, and her love for the town had intensified.

She thought of her wedding to Daniel, a beautiful autumn celebration filled with the quiet reassurance of belonging, and the genuine camaraderie of their close-knit community.

The old Victorian he had lovingly restored for them became a refuge, a place where their love could grow and flourish with each passing day. Not only did his project restore the house, but it also taught him how to channel his creativity and passion for renovation. He told Olivia that he had discovered a purpose and fulfillment that he had never known before.

She remembered Theodore and Lillian's summer wedding, a fairy-tale affair held in the gardens of the Beaumont estate. The once-lost lovers exchanged their sacred words beneath a canopy of twinkling lights, their faces radiant. Olivia caught sight of the tears glistening in Theodore's eyes as he sealed his union with Lillian.

Their marriage sparked a remarkable transformation in both of them.

Theodore, once a man of guarded emotions, now exuded a quiet confidence and a readiness to embrace life. His poetry, consistently poignant, acquired a fresh depth and richness. And Lillian, renowned for her grace and composure, emanated an inner contentment and a profound appreciation for the winding path that brought her back to her true love.

The heart of the town was Emma's bakery, a place where friends converged, relishing in conversation, chuckles, and the irresistible aroma of scones baked to perfection. The tinkling of the bell above the door announced each arrival, and the gentle hum of the espresso machine invited patrons to linger. The heavenly blend of cinnamon, vanilla, and caramelized sugar embraced each visitor as soon as they stepped inside *Blissful Bites.*

Olivia appreciated the strength of her friendship with Emma, a bond that grew stronger with each passing month.

Nora's book club thrived, bringing together readers of all ages and backgrounds to share their passion for literature and the impact of a captivating narrative. Elliot had unexpectedly left Nora after he'd received an inheritance, and she'd been devastated, though seemed to be slowly recovering.

"Don't ask me to try to figure out where he went," Olivia had declared. "Solving one mystery in this town is enough for me."

Meanwhile, Delilah, the eccentric and endearing matchmaker, continued to spread her unique brand of wisdom, reminding everyone of the wonders waiting to be uncovered, even in the smallest instances.

However, the love that Daniel and Olivia had built was the most precious gift of all. While looking at a photograph of her grandparents on their wedding day, Olivia recognized her own story. Just as Elijah and Rachel sculpted a life filled with steadfast commitment, serenity, and endless curiosity, so did Olivia and Daniel.

As if on cue, he appeared in the doorway, a small,

wrapped package in his hands. "I found this on the doorstep, Ollie. It's addressed to you."

She peeled away the layers of brown paper, a flutter of excitement stirring as she recognized Lillian's graceful script on the note tucked inside.

"My dearest Olivia," the note read. "Thank you for restoring the magic in my life. You are the reason Theodore and I rediscovered each other, and because of this, I am eternally grateful. Please accept this small token of my affection and know that you will always hold a special place in my heart. With love, Lillian Weatherly."

Inside the package, Olivia found a silver bracelet, each charm a tiny book engraved with the titles of classic novels.

"This is lovely," Daniel said.

"Yes, it is." Tears of gratitude filled Olivia's eyes as he enveloped her in his arms.

As the stars twinkled in the Pacific Northwest sky, they made their way home, their hearts overflowing with the promise of a lifetime. The cool evening breeze carried with it the faint scent of pine and cherry blossoms, a reminder of the town's timeless charm. She reminisced about the countless evenings she and Daniel spent on their porch swing, sipping tea, and sharing their dreams for the future.

Hand in hand, they walked along the cobblestone, the stones still warm from the day's sun.

And though Elijah and Rachel were no longer with Olivia in person, their guidance would forever be a part of her story, woven into her life.

The curtain fell on another perfect day in Sweetwater Springs, and the streets reverberated with love and laughter. And for Olivia, Daniel, Theodore, Lillian, and all the other beloved residents of this charming town, the future shone brightly with endless possibilities.

A piece of paper dropped out of Lillian's envelope that Olivia had failed to notice, and she stooped to pick it up. From the elongated curves and artistic loops, she recognized Theodore's handwriting. A poem. She read it aloud to Daniel.

"To Olivia and Daniel, the matchmakers, bold, Your story's a tale that deserves to be told.

With whispers of love, you brought Lillian to me, And now, thanks to you, we're a pair meant to be.

So here's to you both, and the joy that you bring, May your own story be a beautiful thing.

With laughter and grace, may you dance through your days, And cherish each moment, in a million small ways.

For in Sweetwater Springs, where the whispers are sweet, And the love stories bloom, from the head to the feet,

You'll always be known as the couple so clever, Who brought two old hearts back together forever."

Love from your dear friend, Theodore."

Olivia folded the poem carefully, a soft smile playing on her lips. She glanced up at Daniel, his eyes shining with the same love that filled her heart.

In the comfortable silence that followed, she realized that the whispers of love in Sweetwater Springs were not a romantic notion, but a fundamental truth. They were present in the unassuming moments of kindness and compassion, and in the quiet strength of a community that always looked out for its own.

As they stepped out into the evening air, the familiar sounds and scents of their beloved town enveloped them. The whispers of love were there, too, in the hush of the leaves and the calm breeze that carried the assurance of a brilliant future.

Hand in hand, Olivia and Daniel walked down the street.

As long as they had each other, they could face anything. And in the end, that was what mattered most.

THE END

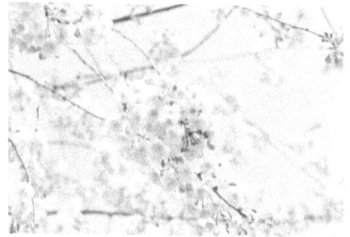

A NOTE FROM JOSIE

Dear Reader,

Thank you for reading *Whispers of Love in Sweetwater Springs*, my sweet romance (with a touch of suspense!) This is the first book in my Sweetwater Springs series, and set in a fictional town in the Pacific Northwest.

I've always been fascinated by how history can shape the present, and how long-buried secrets and forgotten loves can resurface when we least expect them. In *Whispers of Love in Sweetwater Springs*, I wanted to explore the idea that sometimes the key to unlocking our future lies in the mysteries of the past.

As you follow Olivia and Daniel's journey to uncover the truth behind a long-lost love letter, I hope you'll love the charm of Sweetwater Springs. This quaint little town is more than a backdrop. It's a character in its own right, filled with quirky, lovable residents, shared histories and intertwined destinies.

Even in the darkest of times, hope and happiness can be

found if we're willing to open our hearts and take a chance on the unexpected.

Thank you for joining me on this journey, and I can't wait to share more stories from Sweetwater Springs with you in the future!

Warmest wishes,

Josie Riviera

P.S. I'd love to hear your thoughts! Please feel free to reach out to me on social media or via email to share your feedback, ask questions, or say hello. Connecting with readers is one of the greatest joys of being an author, and I'm always thrilled to hear from you.

Whispers of Love in Sweetwater Springs is available in ebook, paperback, Large Print paperback, audiobook, and Hardcover.

P.S. As I write my next sweet or inspirational romance, remember this: Have you ever tried something you were afraid to try because it mattered so much to you? I did, when I started writing. Take the chance, and just do something you love.

Love music?

My Spotify list for Whispers of Love in Sweetwater Springs is here.

RECIPE FOR GRANDMOTHER RACHEL'S DEVILED EGGS

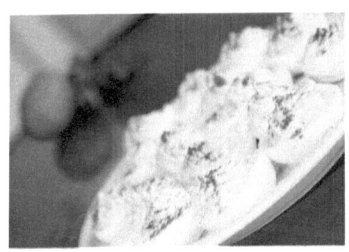

Ingredients:
- 6 large eggs
- 3 tablespoons mayonnaise
- 1 teaspoon Dijon mustard
- 1/2 teaspoon smoked paprika
- Salt and pepper to taste
- Chopped fresh chives or parsley for garnish (optional)

Instructions:

1. Place the eggs in a single layer in a saucepan and cover them with cold water. Bring the water to a

boil over medium-high heat. Once boiling, cover the saucepan with a lid, remove it from the heat, and let the eggs sit in the hot water for 10-12 minutes.

2. After the eggs have cooked, transfer them to a bowl of ice water to cool for about 5 minutes. This will make them easier to peel.

3. Once the eggs are cool enough to handle, carefully peel them under cold running water to help remove the shells.

4. Cut each egg in half lengthwise, and carefully remove the yolks, placing them in a separate bowl. Set the egg whites aside on a serving platter.

5. Mash the yolks with a fork until they are smooth and crumbly. Add the mayonnaise, Dijon mustard, smoked paprika, salt, and pepper to the mashed yolks. Mix everything together until well combined and creamy.

6. Spoon or pipe the yolk mixture back into the egg white halves, dividing it evenly among them.

7. Sprinkle a little extra smoked paprika on top of each deviled egg for garnish.

8. If desired, sprinkle chopped fresh chives or parsley over the eggs for added flavor and color.

9. Serve immediately or refrigerate until ready to serve.

Enjoy your delicious smoked paprika deviled eggs as a tasty appetizer or snack!

BONUS SNEAK PEEK: WHISPERS OF MAPLE MEMORIES IN SWEETWATER SPRINGS CHAPTER ONE PREVIEW

CHAPTER ONE

The map Nora Winters had found hinted at secrets of past truths and a mystery waiting to be solved.

"I don't know what to make of it, Olivia." Nora wrapped her hands around a steaming mug of green tea, her feet tucked beneath her in a cushioned armchair. She and Olivia sat across from each other in a snug corner of *Harper's Haven*, the bookshop that Olivia Whitfield owned.

Nora's visit to the shop had prompted an invitation to sit for a while and chat. The sweet aroma of freshly baked cinnamon rolls wafted through the air, mingling with the scent of old books. Outside, the cheerful clang of the antique bell from Sweetwater Springs' lone firetruck echoed down Main Street, signaling the start of the volunteer firefighter's weekly drill. Children on bicycles pedaled past, their laughter carried on the breeze.

Often, the women shared tea and quiet conversation, particularly after Nora's book club meetings. Today, however, was not about the book club.

Olivia shot Nora a questioning look. "You don't know what to make about what?"

"The map I discovered." Nora stared into her mug and inhaled deeply, letting the mild aroma of the tea calm her nerves. "It's reminiscent of a scene straight out of those whodunit novels you read from cover to cover."

Olivia toyed with the pearl necklace she always wore around her throat.

"Puzzles. I like puzzles," she clarified. "Mystery novels are another issue entirely." A shadow passed over her features, a fleeting hint of reluctance in her brown eyes.

Nora knew why. The investigation into cracking a mystery that Olivia had undertaken had taken a toll on her. She still carried the weight of that experience.

"There's a way to enjoy the thrill of mysteries without the pressure of figuring them out," Nora hastened to assure Olivia. "Take Cozies, for instance, where the riddles are fascinating but not overwhelming."

"Exactly what are you getting at?" Olivia glanced up at the murmur of patrons. They perused the shelves for one last book to take home before the shop closed for the evening. "What map?"

"The map I found in the library was in a book, *The Natural Wonders of Washington State*, written in the early 20th century." Nora set her mug on a side table, then retrieved a folded map from the pocket of her cardigan sweater. The map's faded parchment and fragile edges hinted at years spent tucked away, and intricate lines crisscrossed the surface.

A small 'X,' nearly hidden, was indicated by a dark shade of green. She hadn't noticed it earlier.

"What does the X mean?" She murmured, her mind trying to sort anything she might've overlooked. She unfolded the map and held it up. "This charts a section of Sweetwater Springs, deep in the maple woods."

"Curious." Olivia tucked a strand of chestnut brown hair behind her ear. "The oddest part is the inscription at the bottom. 'In the roots of the past, the truth shall be revealed.'" As she read aloud, she traced the words with her fingers. "What kind? Maple tree roots?"

"That's what I'm wondering." Nora twisted, her gaze gravitating to the floor-to-ceiling bookcase. Fortunately, all the patrons were preoccupied—either deeply engrossed in the latest bestseller or reading back covers.

Maybe the explanation for the inscription was written in a book. Or maybe it could only be found by physically following the map's trail.

"Wherever this leads, it will have an impact. On me, and all of Sweetwater Springs," Nora said.

"Enlighten me, please." Olivia sat back, looking as if she had all the time in the world. "That's a heavy assertion."

Nora hesitated, trying to put her feeling into words. "Perhaps the map is a key to something bigger."

"How?"

"I'm not sure. Are you up for helping me solve it?"

"Me? No." Olivia quickly relayed her escapade as a matchmaker to an older couple in the community. The entire town had witnessed the reunion. A happily ever after all around.

"Theodore and Lillian finally found their way back to each other after decades apart," Olivia continued. "However, I'm done with mysteries. Done with a capital D."

"Sorry to interrupt, but did I hear the word 'mystery'?" Daniel Whitfield entered from the back room, carrying an armful of books. He shook back his dark, wavy hair and grinned.

"Your favorite word. Mystery," Olivia teased with a smile. "Surely your ears are ringing."

"My favorite word is you, Ollie." His gaze warmed; his eyes filled with a tender affection for his wife that spoke volumes of his love for her.

The sharp contrast between Olivia and Daniel's relationship, and Nora's past with Elliot Fitzwater hit Nora as she took in the couple—there was such devotion between them. Absolute happiness. Would she ever know that kind of love, a love that lasted?

Olivia's smile stayed on Daniel as she waved him over. "Nora found an old map in a library book that leads to the maple woods. I've never been there."

Daniel greeted Nora, set the books on a counter, and kissed Olivia on the forehead. "Me neither. Have you ever been there, Nora?"

"Several times, mostly when I was young." Nora didn't elaborate. As usual, Elliot Fitzwater came to mind. They'd visited the maple woods together.

He'd promised he'd make maple syrup with her. The

grove was their special place. They'd find a bigleaf maple tree and tap the tree, drill a hole, insert the tap, and hang a collection bucket. That was only the beginning of the process, though it was typical Elliot.

Big dreams.

Big promises that came to naught.

Months earlier, he'd finally received an inheritance, and with the money, he'd purchased real estate in Austin, Texas. He'd renovated and flipped the properties and capitalized on the increased market demand for sizable profits.

Nora had read about his success story in an entrepreneurial magazine, and he now owned a fancy five thousand square foot home. He also hosted extravagant parties attended by movie stars and business magnates.

Elliot was no longer the fedora-wearing guy from the small town of Sweetwater Springs. Compared to his lavish lifestyle, she felt as simple as a country mouse at a royal ball.

Fortunately, he was no longer a part of her life. He was gone, so why did thoughts of him emerge so frequently? Surely, she should be over him by now.

But she wasn't.

She blinked back tears and looked down. The worn wooden floors blurred, and she dabbed at her eyes. Despite the passage of time, his absence carved a void in her heart that she couldn't seem to fill.

"I've heard whispers about those woods," Daniel was saying as he pulled up a chair beside the women and kissed Olivia again. Both he and his wife were so captivated by each other that neither seemed to notice Nora's tears. "Old stories," he went on, "legends really, about secrets buried deep in the forest."

Nora's posture shifted as she looked up. "What kind of secrets?"

Daniel's shrug was accompanied by a playful glint in

his hazel eyes. "The ultimate question. When you think you've unraveled every story, there's a whisper of the latest hidden treasures and lost loves waiting to be discovered."

"Hidden treasures, huh?" Olivia smirked. "Are you revitalizing your detective mode agenda again?'

Daniel returned Olivia's smirk. "The maple woods hold a legend of long-ago stories."

"Good stories, hopefully." Nora chuckled, a tad too frantically, attempting to conceal her nervousness.

"Mostly," he replied. "Why?"

"I'm worried that I'll find something."

"Like what?"

She needed no further urging. "A conflict or argument, a health concern, financial troubles ..."

"All because of a map? I hardly doubt it."

"News can be bad, right?"

"News can also be good." Daniel replied. "They claim that if you listen closely, the stories of the past can still be detected in the rustling leaves."

"Who's they?" Olivia's gaze strayed to a customer at the cash register, and she quickly stood. "I've never heard anything of the sort. You're in quite a mood today, Mr. Whitfield."

"What kind of mood, Mrs. Whitfield?"

"You've been reading too many detective novels. You're becoming a deep thinker."

He winked. "So, I am."

"Even so, he might be right." Olivia squeezed Nora's hand, her lighthearted expression turning serious, clearly meant to temper any of Nora's impulsive plans. "If you plan to pursue this, please be careful."

"What about you two?" Nora asked. "Will you help?"

"We're here for you."

Nora glanced between her friends, thankful for their support.

Olivia and Daniel had married the previous autumn. As newlyweds and both running businesses, they had enough concerns without piling on another to their already full days.

Olivia's brows furrowed. "This reminds me of the suspenseful novel series I've been cataloging. The one about the librarian turned detective."

Daniel chuckled. "Only you would find a literary reference in all this, Ollie. Remember how rattled you were after Theodore and Lillian's mystery?"

Olivia swatted his arm. "I wasn't rattled. I was ... invigorated."

"Is that what we're calling it now? Invigorated?" he teased.

Nora watched their easy banter with a blend of fondness and envy. Their connection was undeniable. Olivia's quiet strength complemented Daniel's easygoing nature perfectly.

"If you're determined to pursue this, Nora," Olivia said, straightening the sleeves of her vintage blouse, "we'll help however we can. Daniel's research skills are unparalleled, and I suppose I might dust off my amateur sleuthing hat."

Daniel raised an eyebrow. "Ollie, need I remind you of the Sweetwater Springs Bake Sale Caper of 98?"

"There was no such thing."

"Mrs. Henderson's prize-winning blackberry pie recipe was at stake."

"Absolutely not."

As they laughed, Nora felt a wave of gratitude. Whatever this mystery held, she could count on Olivia's sharp mind and Daniel's steady support.

"I won't bother you unless I really need you," she assured.

Olivia smoothed her long wool skirt, then skirted to the counter to greet the growing line of customers. "You're never a bother," she said over her shoulder.

Nora turned over the map. Two corners had marks, barely visible unless you looked closely.

"Daniel, do you see these?" she asked.

"Yeah. They're not on every corner."

"The marks can mean nothing, but …"

"In a mystery, nothing is ever really nothing," he said with a smile.

Her decision made, Nora stood and brushed the hem of her red knit dress. "Tomorrow, I'll stop by the maple grove after work."

"It'll be dark by then," Daniel said.

"I'm done at noon. Tonight, I'm preparing for the adult education class I'm teaching."

She'd designed the class to foster a love for reading and to improve literacy skills. Several adults attended, ranging from those looking to improve their reading, to others wanting to enhance their English proficiency.

With a determined nod at both Daniel and Olivia, she brought her mug into the back room, then pulled on her waterproof jacket and chunky knit scarf.

As she left the warmth of *Harper's Haven* and stepped outside, the sky had turned a midnight blue, signaling the approach of nightfall. The crunch of fallen leaves underfoot mixed with the distant aroma of burning firewood, a reminder of snug evenings lost in the pages of a beloved book. A typical fall day in the Pacific Northwest, with a persistent gentle drizzle.

A maple leaf, tinged with the blush of crimson, drifted lazily to the ground, an indication of the transformations to come. Like the leaves, the untold stories of Sweetwater Springs were on the verge of unveiling themselves, waiting for the right person to piece together the fragments of a forgotten history.

She swung the scarf tighter around her, pulled the hood

of her jacket over her head, and patted the map tucked securely in her pocket.

Were there really secrets hidden in the maple woods, promising answers to questions she hadn't even known to ask?

The muted glow of the streetlights guided her, reminding passersby to seek refuge from the brisk bite of the season in their comfy, intimate homes.

Nora had no such home. Despite the familiar furnishings and the comforting presence of her belongings, her apartment on Meadowlark Lane stood as a silent witness to her solitude. The photograph of her and Elliot, tucked away in a bureau in her living room, whispered of a love that had slipped through her fingers.

She walked along the cobblestone streets, the worn stones gleaming like river-polished gems after a recent rain shower. The tang of wood smoke mingled with the sweet aroma of ripe blackberries from Mrs. Henderson's overgrown bushes. The town's clock tower chimed the hour, its deep resonance vibrating through the soles of her boots, while a flock of starlings swooped overhead.

When she made the last turn to her apartment, a blur of motion burst from a townhouse. A young boy came careening past her on his bicycle. Hot on his heels was his mother, a dark-haired Latina woman.

"Santiago!" the woman called, chuckling as she raced after him. "Give me back my book! I need it for Miss Winters' class."

The boy waved a recognizable leather-bound book in the air, keeping it out of her reach.

Nora recognized the woman from her adult reading class. She observed the lively exchange, outmaneuvered Santiago's defense, and snatched the book from him.

"Don't forget to help your mother with her assignment, okay, Santiago?" she asked.

"Okay, Miss Winters." He hesitated. "You're really pretty."

"Thank you."

"Can I date you when I get older?"

"When you're eighteen, I assure you that you'll be happier with someone closer to your own age." With a fond smile, she playfully tugged his knit cap down over his ears. "Here's your book, Mrs. Ruiz." Nora handed the book back to the woman. "Are you enjoying the material for our class?"

"The self-help manual lists strategies I didn't realize I needed. I look forward to our next session."

Nora smiled, turned her attention to the mother and son departing, and then entered her apartment a few minutes later. She removed her waterproof boots, then shrugged off her jacket and hung it on a rack near the door.

She regarded her kitchen, where shiny copper pans and pots dangled gracefully from hooks on the wall. The polished surfaces reflected the glow of the under-cabinet lights. Although she enjoyed cooking, creating a mess to cook fettuccini Alfredo for one person seemed more effort than it was worth.

Opting for a toasted cheese sandwich instead, she tidied the counter, then wandered into the living room. She watered her thriving, tall palms, then switched on a lamp. As she settled into her favorite armchair, she reached for the remote and turned on a small vintage radio.

The opening chords of *The Story*, by Brandi Carlile, filled the space, and Nora hummed along. Listening to the lyrics, she reflected on her own journey.

"All of these lines across my face tell you who I am," Brandi crooned, and Nora outlined the subtle lines at the corners of her own eyes.

Each experience had left its mark, shaping her into the

woman she'd become. With a smile, she took a bite of her sandwich and eyed the stack of teaching materials on her antique bureau.

Although she told herself she shouldn't, she stood and tugged a photograph out of the top drawer of her bureau. Her fingers quivered. She fixed her gaze on the image, and the world faded away as she stared at the man she had loved.

The memories were too painful to revisit, but here she was, and there was no hope for her lack of self-control.

The photograph reflected a happier moment—her and Elliot at the annual Sweetwater Springs potluck supper. She'd brought a chicken and vegetable stew that had simmered for hours in his aunt Delilah's kitchen.

Aunt Delilah. Wow, she was quite a character.

Elliot looked so handsome with his chiseled features and prominent cheekbones. That night, he'd worn a blue linen button-down shirt and olive-green chinos that accentuated his slim build.

Her own face beamed back at her behind horn-rimmed eyeglasses; her brown eyes gleaming with a joy she hardly recognized.

The red floral dress she'd worn mocked her, a reminder of the confidence and expectations she had once possessed. She loved that dress—the fitted bodice and flowing skirt. Bold and empowered, she'd assured herself that there was truly such a thing as a fairy-tale ending.

Of course, there wasn't any such thing. At least, not for her.

Those days were gone, the boldness, the empowerment when her world seemed filled with endless possibilities. Those qualities were from a distant past she'd never reclaim.

Her relationship with Elliot had been a whirlwind of highs and lows, fueled by love and misunderstandings. She recalled the quiet promises, the laughter as they explored

Sweetwater Springs together. Along with those memories were episodes of hurt, and wounds that still simmered below the surface.

If she ever saw him again, how could she ever forgive him?

With a heavy sigh, she slid the photograph back into the drawer, silently acknowledging the pieces of her heart she had given away the night Elliot had proclaimed his love, and she had declared her love for him.

Forcibly reminding herself that he'd left soon afterwards, she'd donated her dress to Goodwill. She could always shop at Goodwill and buy her dress back, she told herself. She never had, just as she'd never reclaimed her heart.

The fog of distraction that plagued her ever since she discovered the map gave way to a sharp awareness. The empty spaces between her furniture pieces served as a constant reminder of her loneliness. Each room was a silent witness to her solitary existence.

She cast off her self-pity and whispered with a broken laugh, "Enough time has passed. We're both in our thirties now, and I really need to start dating again."

She pulled her sandy-brown hair from her slicked back bun and let the shiny mass fall over her shoulders. Her teaching materials beckoned, though concentration eluded her.

She settled into her favorite armchair again and spread the map out before her. She thought about Daniel's description of love and loss. Was the map steering her to a long-forgotten story?

The memory of Elliot's devastating smile rushed through her mind, quick and unexpected, and she pushed it away. She made a silent vow to seek the truth of the maple woods. Perhaps, in doing so, she'd find peace. Perhaps she'd even summon the courage to unlock her heart again.

Just as Nora was winding down for the evening, a rapid knock at the door jolted her. Cautiously, she ventured to the entrance of her apartment and swung the door open, greeted by the oversized smile of Delilah Fitzwater, Elliot's flamboyant aunt and Sweetwater Springs' resident matchmaker extraordinaire. Ironically, Delilah, a vibrant woman in her 60s, was a matchmaker who had never married.

Her clothes were a riot of color—her hair was topped by a purple feather boa, which didn't suit the chilly weather. Then again, this was Aunt Delilah. A blizzard could've swirled around her, and she would've continued to dress outrageously.

"Aunt Delilah! I was just thinking about you." Nora blinked. Her hand fluttered to her face. "Is it okay ... if I still call you, my aunt?"

"Ooh, of course, sugar plum."

"What brings you here at this hour? I haven't seen you in ages."

"What an exquisite tiny apartment!" Delilah breezed in and sniffed. "And it smells so fresh."

"Umm. Come on in. You're probably smelling the plants from my herb garden."

"Ah, yes." Delilah practically bounced into the living room, taking in the furniture, crafted from reclaimed wood, and complemented by plush pillows.

"I simply couldn't wait until tomorrow! I was at *Harper's Haven* earlier today and overheard your conversation with Olivia and Daniel about the intriguing map you found."

Nora raised an eyebrow. "You were at the bookshop?"

"I'm always on the hunt for the latest romance novels, although that's not why I'm here. The maple woods triggered a memory of a story my grandmother once shared with me."

Despite the late hour, well past nine o'clock in the evening, Nora relaxed, though playing the polite hostess was a bit of a chore. Yet, she wanted to prolong the visit because Delilah Fitzwater was Elliot's aunt, and her presence somehow brought Elliot closer, as if he were in Nora's apartment again.

She hung Delilah's bright-purple raincoat on a coat rack, then motioned for her to take a seat on the sofa. "Care for a cup of mint tea?" she asked graciously.

Delilah flattened her flowing printed skirt. "Mint tea is lovely. Thanks."

Nora brewed the tea at lightning speed, placed china cups and saucers and a teapot on a wooden tray, and returned to the living room.

"For whatever reason, I'm nervous," she admitted, setting the tray on the coffee table. The table, made from a repurposed barn door, held a stack of art magazines and a hand-crafted ceramic bowl filled with apples.

Delilah's gaze landed on the apples. "May I have one?"

"Of course."

Bringing the apple to her lips, Delilah inhaled. "Now tell me why you're nervous."

"Because you're Elliot's aunt and all."

"Although I'm related to Elliot, I'm obviously not Elliot. You're a smart and caring woman. There's nothing to be nervous about." The sincerity in Delilah's eyes made Nora feel bold and courageous again, those wonderful feelings that she'd once embraced.

"Thank you. And you're an incredible woman." Nora smiled and cleared her throat. "Before we continue, how is Elliot?"

Ugh, why had she asked that question? She was through with him.

Nonetheless, there was scant point in exchanging pleasantries until the main issue on her mind was addressed. She braced for a condescending, vague answer.

With a satisfying crunch, Delilah sunk her teeth into the apple. Juice dribbled down her chin as she chewed, then swallowed. "Elliot is well. He's surrounded by fashionable, wealthy people."

"I've read as much in the tabloids. We haven't been in contact since he left Sweetwater Springs ... so abruptly."

"He's always been a wanderer, starting when he was a youngster and took to wearing a fedora." Delilah seemed to stall by taking small bites of the apple, then digressing to minor details about Elliot. "The maple trees have a little romance in store for you."

Regretfully, romance was a thing of the past for Nora. "I'll focus on the mystery first, but I'm all ears for your grandmother's tale."

Delilah's exuberant giggle crinkled her green eyes. "My grandmother believed those woods had a way of uniting people."

Nora grinned at the enthusiasm. "Does her story shed any light on the map I found?"

As she reached the apple's core, Delilah inspected it, then paused. "Call it a matchmaker's intuition, but I detect a connection. Many years ago, my grandmother said that the maple woods spoke of love and adventure."

That word again. Love. Didn't Elliot's aunt know that true love between a man and a woman wasn't part of Nora's life anymore? Her mind whirled with question after question, though Delilah's responses usually went off on a tangent. Near the end of the conversation, Nora mentioned that she planned to go to the woods the following afternoon to explore.

"Good idea, sugar plum." Delilah set her apple on a napkin, then poured the last of the tea from the teapot and slurped it down.

A few minutes later, Nora bid Delilah farewell as they

stood on the front porch, waving until Delilah disappeared from view.

With a sigh, she went back inside her apartment and retrieved the photograph of her and Elliot.

"If you ever return to Sweetwater Springs," she murmured. "Don't look me up, because I will never forgive you for leaving me flat."

Read the rest of Nora and Elliot's Story

Pick up your copy of *Whispers of Maple Memories in Sweetwater Springs* today!

FREE on Kindle Unlimited.

*** End of excerpt *Whispers of Maple Memories in Sweetwater Springs* by Josie Riviera
Copyright © 2024 Josie Riviera
***

Also grab: The Sweetwater Springs Series.
Coming in January 2025:

ABOUT THE AUTHOR

Josie Riviera is a *USA TODAY* bestselling author of contemporary, inspirational, and historical sweet romances that read like Hallmark movies. She lives in the Charlotte, NC, area with her wonderfully supportive husband. They share their home with an adorable shih tzu, who constantly needs grooming, and live in an old house forever needing renovations.

To receive my Newsletter and your free sweet romance novella ebook as a thank you gift, sign up HERE.

Become a member of my Read and Review VIP Facebook group for exclusive giveaways and ARCs.

ALSO BY JOSIE RIVIERA

Seeking Patience

Seeking Catherine (always Free!)

Seeking Fortune

Seeking Charity

Seeking Rachel

The Seeking Series

Oh Danny Boy

I Love You More

A Snowy White Christmas

A Portuguese Christmas

Holiday Hearts Book Bundle Volume One

Holiday Hearts Book Bundle Volume Two

Holiday Hearts Book Bundle Volume Three

Holiday Hearts Book Bundle Volume Four

Holiday Hearts Book Bundle Volume Five

Candleglow and Mistletoe

Maeve (Perfect Match)

A Love Song To Cherish

A Christmas To Cherish

A Valentine To Cherish

A Christmas Puppy To Cherish

A Homecoming To Cherish

A Summer To Cherish

Romance Stories To Cherish

Romance Stories To Cherish Volume Two

Cherished Hearts Six Book Volume

Aloha To Love

Sweet Peppermint Kisses

Valentine Hearts Boxed Set

1-800-CUPID

1-800-CHRISTMAS

1-800-IRELAND

1-800-SUMMER

1-800-NEW YEAR

The 1-800-Series Sweet Contemporary Romance Bundle

Irish Hearts Sweet Romance Bundle

Holly's Gift

A Chocolate-Box Christmas

A Chocolate-Box New Years

A Chocolate-Box Valentine

A Chocolate-Box Summer Breeze

A Chocolate-Box Christmas Wish

A Chocolate-Box Irish Wedding

Chocolate-Box Hearts

Chocolate-Box Hearts Volume Two

Chocolate-Box Double Hearts

Recipes From The Heart

Leading Hearts

New Year Hearts

SENIOR HEARTS

Summer Hearts

Christmas in the Air (1-800-Book)

A Very Christian Christmas

The 1-800-Series Volume Two

The 1-800-Series Complete Collection

Christmas Tails of the Heart

Cocoa's Christmas Love

Pawfect Christmas Hearts

Pink Coral Island

Whispers of Love in Sweetwater Springs

Whispers of Maple Memories in Sweetwater Springs

Whispers of Holiday Magic in Sweetwater Springs

Whispers of Sweetwater Springs

A Harvest of Miracles

A Winter Promise

A Season Out of Time

Hearts and Horseshoes

Wishes and Wildflowers

1-800-CUPIDON (French Edition)

1-800-CUPIDO (Spanish Edition)

1-800-AMOR (German Edition)

Most books are available in ebook, audiobook, paperback, Large Print paperback and Hardcover.

Many are FREE on Kindle Unlimited.

PRAISE AND AWARDS

USA TODAY bestselling author

A GIFT FOR YOU

To keep up on newly released ebooks, paperbacks, Large Print Paperbacks, audiobooks, as well as exclusive sales, sign up for Josie's Newsletter today.

As a thank you, I'll send you a Free PDF ... The Beauty Of ...

Josie's Newsletter

Did you know that according to a Yale University study, people who read books live longer?